Thank you for having me!

Deranged

Book 2 of the Fleischer Series

Wendi L. Starusnak

Wendi
Starusnak

ISBN: 149750354X
ISBN-13: 978-1497503540

DISCLAIMER

DEDICATION

I'd like to dedicate Deranged to my loving husband Ron and all of our exceptional children (Ashley, Ronnie, David, Jade, Derrick, Jenna, Laurie, and Luke). They have each taught me so much about life and love while continuing to help me remain grounded in reality, a place I probably would not choose to visit if it weren't for my family. They make each day worth the effort, worth every struggle, and my husband and my children are the reason that I do anything that I do. Without them, Deranged would never have been written. Thank you and I love you all!

NOTE FROM THE AUTHOR

Deranged is a work of fiction. It's not true. There are truths woven throughout, some mine, some belonging to others, and some are just made up. Do things like what happen in Deranged really happen? Yes, unfortunately they do. The main message in Deranged is that abuse is a vicious cycle. This was the main message in Book 1 of the Fleischer Series and will continue to be the main message in Books 3 and 4 as well. You see, abuse feeds on silence and ignorance. Sweep it under the carpet, pretend it doesn't happen, that it's not as bad as it seems or that it could be worse. Pretend that it's not your problem. This is what abuse hungers for, what it needs to continue to haunt little children and grown adults alike. This is how abuse recruits its followers, it creates monsters out of once-beautiful people by putting them through unspeakable torments.

I urge everyone to find their voice, to speak out against abuse when you see it or suspect it, or when it happens to you. Do what that little voice in your heart is begging you to do. It may not be the easy thing to do, anything worth doing rarely is, but it's the right thing to do. You may change someone's life or even save a life, so speak up!

ACKNOWLEDGMENTS

Tasha Gwartney - for an amazing front cover and Dad for an equally amazing back cover,
Bryan Airel- for being my go-to proofreader and putting up with my harassing messages when I'm being impatient,
Amanda Henderson Neally and Doris St Clair- both for agreeing to proofread and giving me such a fast turnaround with glowing feedback,
Crystal Easling – for great last-minute ideas about how to improve Deranged,
Ron Starusnak Jr. - for treating me like a queen every day and for always being my biggest fan,
Christine Vorndran - for being a true friend and for always being there for me in good times and in bad and also for helping me with some of the formatting that I couldn't seem to figure out for the life of me,
Louie Neverette – for also being a true friend and for always being there for me through both the good times and the bad,
Mom & Dad- for reading my manuscript and giving me honest feedback and advice and Dad for help with all the technical stuff,
Grandma Cron- for living a life worthy of a hundred best-selling books and sharing many of her experiences with me.
I give you all my sincere gratitude. I'm truly sorry if I've left anyone out. There are so many people that have given me advice, encouragement, and believed in me along my journey that I couldn't possibly mention all of them here.

LAST CHAPTER OF DETACHED- BOOK
1 OF THE FLEISCHER SERIES

AVAILABLE NOW

~Julie~

It was quite a while before Johnny and Caroline came back home from bringing the produce into town to sell. That seemed to make us a little more money than just selling it roadside in our own yard and had been one of my ideas actually. Dad had finally listened and sent Johnny in his truck with Caroline to try the idea out and see if it really worked. He would never find out the answer, but it would be useful for the rest of us to know for the future.

I had mom seated and positioned the best that I could get her in her chair at the table and dinner was almost finished. Johnny looked around seeming confused and then asked, "Where's Dad? I wanted to show him this catfish I bought at the fish market."

I took him aside where Mom and Caroline wouldn't hear and told him, "He left us Johnny. Just told Mom he was done with us. Hopped in the driver's side of some red head's truck and just sped off."

I could see him trying to let that news sink in. "But that makes no sense."

"Well, that's what happened. Mom's not handling it that well, so try to keep quiet about it." And then louder so that I could be sure everyone would hear, "I made dinner. Something Dad took out this morning. It should be done."

I dished Johnny's bowl and then Caroline's. Then I got Mom's. I was too worn out to be hungry. I took a seat next to Mom and tucked a napkin into her shirt. "Are you going to feed yourself or do I need to do it?" Johnny and Caroline both looked at me in surprise, but kept quiet. There was no answer from our mother. So I picked up the spoon and started to feed her some of the broth from the stew.

She didn't swallow and just let it spill back out of her loose mouth. I let Julie slap her across the face. Not hard, just enough to send a message to wherever she was at in her head. "You have to eat Mother." As I fished some more broth from the bowl, I noticed a big finger hiding in among the vegetables. It looked like a pointer finger. Oops, hopefully I didn't overlook too much of that. The next *spoonful she swallowed. Good. She did the same with most of the rest of the bowl.*

When everyone had finished their suppers and taken their bowls to the sink I asked, "Did I do an alright job with making dinner?"

"That was good," said Caroline, my sweet little sister.

"Good. Don't ever forget what Dad always tells us: don't get too attached..."

Johnny looked directly at me as he finished my sentence for me, "...because it might be supper."

There was a lot to figure out and take care of if Emily and her brother and sister were going to make it look like they weren't on their own in this house. Which, even though their mother was there in body, her mind had certainly taken off to someplace far away.

Emily and Caroline would also have to keep up with their school work. Johnny was old enough now not to have to do the school work any longer. One of them would have to figure out how to do the paperwork for The State.

They would also have to figure out what bills there were and how to pay them. There was a lot, but I knew they would be able to handle it. They had handled far worse when their father was alive.

CHAPTER ONE
Caroline

I close the last journal there is of my sister Emily's, turn out my flashlight, and just sit for a while in the dark, damp cellar, thinking. Emily is her name, whether she likes it or not. I don't know where this whole calling her Julie thing came from. Well, I do now that I've read all of her journals, but it doesn't really make very much sense to me. Did this Julie person, or whatever she is, take over Emily's mind and turn her into this monster that she has become? I don't want Emily, or Julie as she now likes to be called, to find me down here snooping through her private journals. After putting the last of the notebooks back behind the loose brick in the wall where I found them, I decide to go outside for a while.

I was just looking around the room that Daddy had made Emily stay in by herself after he got mad at her. I was thinking about the way that things had gone all wrong that year and had noticed the brick sticking out. I probably should not have read her private journals, but I just couldn't seem to stop myself from opening each journal and then turning each of the pages. Reading the journals made me think about the old Emily and how much I really miss my big sister. It also gave me some idea how she saw the things that had happened and how she had felt about everything.

One of the last things that Daddy ever did before Emily (or Julie) killed him was to cut some of the branches back on the old willow tree in our yard. Emily was really upset about that, but he did it so that he could hang a swing for us in the tree. He did it mostly for me, since I'm the youngest kid now.

I remember that day so clearly. I was so happy and Daddy was in such a good mood too. I love my swing, even after what happened in this tree, and I spend a lot of time here just sitting and thinking. I only sit because I don't really know how to swing. Daddy told me that he would teach me but he didn't get a chance to before he was killed, and then Mommy wasn't herself at all after he died. Johnny doesn't have the time to spend trying to teach me something so unimportant and I don't even want to ask Julie to teach me.

It's really nice out today. The sun is shining so bright and I can hear the birds chirping away loudly. They sound excited that spring is finally back again. I'm happy about that too. Now I can get out of the house. I can try to stay away from the mean person that my sister has turned into since she told me and Johnny that Daddy ran off with another woman. Now I know the horrible, disgusting truth. We ate our Daddy for supper that awful night.

I'm scared of this wicked Julie that Emily changed into

so suddenly. She's not like my older sister used to be at all. She's mean and only seems to care about herself. So I guess in some ways it is only right that we call her by a different name now, since she does act like a completely different person.

So much has changed since Daddy has been gone. Things aren't better around here, just very different. Like me calling our father Daddy. Julie screams at me for talking about him at all and when I do and I call him Daddy, she smacks me. She hits me when I call her Emily too. Johnny doesn't even try to stop her. I think that he's afraid of this Julie too.

Julie moved my room to the room that Mommy and Daddy had shared together. She said she doesn't ever want anything to do with anything that used to be theirs. I don't mind at all. The bed is big and more comfortable than mine was and I have a dresser all to myself that even has a mirror above it. I feel closer to Mommy and Daddy here too. I know they were mean and did bad things, but they were still my mommy and daddy and I miss them every single day. Plus, having their room means that I don't have to share my room with meanie Julie anymore.

Julie has the bedroom that Emily and I had always shared all to herself now. Emily meant for her new baby to sleep in that room with her when it came. If it was a boy she said she was going to call him Eric, after our dead brother. She never did say what she would call it if it was a girl. She took the cradle out of the barn that Daddy built when Mommy was pregnant for Johnny and put it up there in our old room before the baby was born.

I asked Emily if she was happy that she was going to have a baby. She thought for a minute before answering me and then told me that it wasn't something that she would have chosen to do, but that it was what it was and she loved her baby already and would take the best care of him or her that she could.

I was proud of Emily for that. I think that it is very important that every kid knows what it's like to be loved. My mommy and daddy loved all of us, I know they did. Emily loved me too but she didn't believe that our parents really loved us.

I was kind of excited about Emily's baby coming. She told me that I would be Aunt Caroline to her baby and that I could help her take care of him or her sometimes. Emily said that I could even watch the baby while she did the chores that needed to be done. I would have loved that baby so much and taken such good care of it.

Each of us kids had slept in the cradle that Emily had brought up to her room when we were babies. Mommy would tell us such nice stories about how Daddy had gone and chopped the wood that he needed to make the cradle, how he worked so hard to shape each piece, and how he nailed and screwed each piece carefully together. After it was all put together and sanded down, Mommy said that she painted the cradle for us. Mommy talked about how proud Daddy had been of himself for being able to make such a beautiful piece of furniture. Emily kept her dead baby in the cradle in her room for a few days with her, until he started to stink too much. Then we buried him in the flower garden that I planted, right next to where our little brother Eric is buried.

So much has happened since that spring in the year 1976. I think about all the terrible things, and the very few good things, that happened a lot. Well, I think about them all of the time really. I have nothing new or exciting to think about. I have nothing to look forward to, nothing better to think about than the past and the few good times that our family had when we were all still together. Mostly the year that everything really started to change, 1976, goes through my head, along with the long years between then and now.

We ate our pet horse one night for dinner. I think that's when it all really started getting bad; life for us Fleischer's, that is. Whisper didn't really taste that bad, but I guess it was just the idea that we ate something that we loved and cared about that made it so horrible.

Daddy said that he had to do it. He never told us why he had to do it. Something was probably wrong with Whisper to make Daddy kill her and he had always taught us kids that it was better to make good use of something if you can, rather than let it go to waste.

I'm glad Whisper's life wasn't for nothing and that we ate her instead of letting her body rot after she was no good even for riding. I knew how to ride a little. I'm not very good at it yet and I probably never will be, but I had ridden Whisper once or twice before she had to die.

Our little brother Eric died suddenly one night and we buried him the next day in the backyard. That was really hard and really sad for me. I don't know what happened to him. I know Emily's journal said it was Daddy's fault, but I think she just made that story up to have someone to blame. All I know is that Eric is gone now and he's never going to come back. I think I miss him even more than I miss Mommy and Daddy. Me and Eric would always play together whenever we got the chance and we could complain to each other about whatever we wanted without having to worry about the other one tattling.

I remember this one time we both almost got ourselves into a world of trouble because of Eric. Somehow we managed to weasel our way completely out of the whole situation though. Eric hadn't felt good and was having trouble getting his share of the chores done. So when I was all done with my chores for the day, I tried to help him get his finished as fast as we could. We accidentally let the pigs out of their pen while we were feeding them their slop and were chasing them around the yard when Mommy caught us. I explained to her that Eric was sick and that I was only trying to help him get his chores done more quickly so that he could go to bed. She felt sorry for Eric and got Johnny and Emily to help us catch the pigs and get them back in their pen before Daddy found out. He would have taken the belt to our bare bottoms for sure if he had heard about it.

I wonder what Eric would be like if he were still alive now? Would everything else that happened still have happened if he didn't die? Sometimes I still get mad at him for leaving me behind the way that he did. I know it wasn't his fault, but I just can't help it. Hot tears are starting to roll down my cheeks just thinking about my little brother and how very much I miss him. My heart aches thinking of everything and everyone that I have lost. I wish that I had died with one of them instead of being stuck here almost on my own.

In the year 1976, while all the bad things were happening, I also made my very first and only friend. Her name was Summer. Was. She even spent the night at our house one night with me. We had so much fun that night, me and Summer. We played dolls together and talked a whole bunch about anything and everything that there was to talk about.

She told me all about regular school and the things that other kids get to do there. She also talked about all the other kids that go there. It all sounded like so much fun to me. I've never been to a regular school and I've never really gotten to spend any time with other kids, besides the little bit of time that I got to spend with Summer.

Something else that she told me that stuck in my head was something that Summer's class had done the last year that she went to school. Each of the thirty-three kids in Summer's class had put something special of their own in a shoebox that the teacher had brought in. Summer told me that she had put a picture of her mother and her together in the shoebox. Then they had buried it in the school yard for someone else to find and dig up years later. She said that her teacher had called the shoebox filled with everybody's special items a time capsule.

Summer and I had talked about burying our very own time capsule together. We never got a chance to do that though. Now that I'm thinking about it, I should put together my own time capsule and bury it so that maybe someday someone will find it and all of the things that I decide to put inside. Summer had thought that maybe she would be the one to dig up her class's box when she was a grown up and to find all the special little things that each of the students had left. Neither one of us knew then what was going to happen to her, that my only friend would never even get a chance to grow up.

Daddy killed my only friend Summer and her mommy after we brought Summer home. He told me to stay in the truck but I got scared because he was gone so long and went into the big apartment building to find him anyway. I followed the sound of Daddy's voice to Summer's apartment door. I opened her door without knocking because I could hear Daddy through the door saying, "See what you made me do?" That's when I saw him leaning over both of their bleeding bodies.

I still don't know why he did that. I was very mad at him for a long time for doing that. I thought a lot about why he would have done something like that to my friend. Maybe Summer said something bad about me or someone else in our family to her mommy. Or maybe she said something mean about our house. I guess I'll never really know why he did what he did and I guess it doesn't even matter that much anymore.

I haven't even tried to make any more friends since then. I haven't really had any chances to make any new friends even if I wanted to. But I decided that day that I never wanted another friend for the rest of my whole life. Something bad always seems to happen to anyone that I care anything about.

Sometime during that same year, Daddy made Emily kill our dog and then we ate him for supper, just like we had eaten our pet horse. Daddy told us that Emily said some terrible lies about him to Mommy so he had to teach her a lesson. He said that Mommy almost ran away and left all of us behind because of the rotten things that Emily said.

I didn't want to eat Lucky because I loved him so much, but Daddy had said if I didn't then Lucky would think that I hated him. I didn't want Lucky to think that, so I ate. I was really angry at Emily for being so bad. It was all her fault that our dog had to die and that we had to eat him for supper. It wasn't very yummy at all and I had to force myself to keep eating without barfing, but I managed to eat it all so that I wouldn't get in trouble.

When he was still alive, Daddy did things to me that hurt my girl parts. He had been doing those things ever since I could first remember. He said he was trying to teach me to be strong and that he only did it because he loved me. I knew that he loved me and he told me those were our special times together that should be a secret love between only him and me. He made me promise not to tell anyone about our special love. I tried not to cry but I couldn't help it, it always hurt so much.

One time he made me, Johnny, and Emily do the bad things with each other. I didn't like that at all. It didn't hurt as much as when Daddy did the stuff with me by himself, but I didn't like the others to be a part of it. I didn't feel so special when they were there too.

I read in Emily's journals that there was a little girl and her mommy in the barn for a while that I never knew about. I'm glad I didn't know anything about that. The journal said that Emily and Johnny helped Daddy take them from the playground in town and then Daddy did bad things to them and killed them.

I do know that a policeman came around one day asking Daddy questions and Daddy killed him out in the barn. I saw Daddy running back from the barn that day looking so scared. Daddy said it was because the policeman was trying to take him from us and he couldn't let that happen. No cops have ever come back since then to ask any questions about anything. It's too late for that little girl and her mommy now anyways. What was done is done and they are gone. At least they don't have to live a lonely life like mine.

One afternoon during that awful year, Daddy burned an "F" into my butt cheek and everyone else's in the family. That was probably the most painful thing I have ever been through in my life. I was sore for what seemed like forever after. Emily rubbed Aloe from our plant on the hurt spot for me for several days after, and I did the same for her. It's all better now though.

Now I have a scar that's shaped in the form of the letter "F". So do Julie and Johnny. Now that it doesn't hurt anymore, I think it's actually kind of neat that all of us have matching scars. Daddy had called them our brands.

Late in the summer of 1976, we were supposed to go to the State Fair for the first time ever, but me and Emily never ended up going. Emily made herself and me real sick instead. I thought we were both going to die, that's how sick she made us. She told me at the time that it was because Daddy had something really bad planned for when we were supposed to be there.

I read in her journal exactly what Johnny had told her was supposed to happen. Daddy was supposed to sell us to other men so they could do bad things to us. I really wanted to go and I still wonder if Johnny and Emily just lied to get me sick and make me not go. I do know that Mommy and Daddy were arguing really loud when they got back from the Fair that day though. Maybe someday I'll get to the Fair myself, but my time is running out, and honestly, I don't really care anymore whether I ever get to go to the Fair or not. The only people that I would have liked to go with are gone forever.

Emily, or Julie, killed Daddy and we ate him for supper not long after we celebrated my ninth birthday. It was right before Halloween, the same year that Eric died. Julie tried telling me and Johnny that Daddy had run off with another woman, but I kind of knew in my head even then that he would never do something like that to us. Daddy was always telling us how important family was and how we needed to stick together no matter what. Plus, I know that Daddy really loved each and every one of us.

I have a really hard time thinking about how Daddy was killed and what Daddy must have gone through just before he died. Also, I don't like to think about the fact that I actually ate part of my own father. I read the awful truth about what happened to him in Emily's journal and almost threw up right then and there because of it.

Mommy didn't act like herself after Daddy was gone. She didn't do anything anymore. She wouldn't talk to us or cook or clean. She didn't even dress or feed herself anymore. She just kind of sat around, when Julie actually bothered to get her out of her bed.

If Julie didn't feel like getting her out of bed, Mommy would just stay laying there all day, staring up at her ceiling. There was always a look on her face like she was far away somewhere else. I wonder where she imagined she was and why she wouldn't choose to stay with us instead. Didn't she care about us as at least as much as she cared about Daddy? She wasn't like Mommy at all anymore, just like Emily is now Julie.

Then one day I walked outside and found Mommy hanging by a rope around her neck right next to my swing. The horror of seeing my mother swinging by her neck in that tree was beyond words. It was so unbelievably terrible that I just tried to erase it from my mind, as if I never saw it. Truthfully, that is the only way that I have been able to keep myself from going totally crazy.

I pretend a lot. So, instead of seeing my poor dead mother like that over and over again inside my head, I try really hard to pretend that all I can see is my swing. Sometimes it works, but sometimes, like when I'm trying to go to sleep at night, I picture Mommy hanging dead in the tree. Sometimes it gets even worse and she lifts her head and opens her eyes to try to talk to me. I shut my eyes as tight as I can and try to think of anything but the scary things that are inside my head.

I call the swing my swing because no one else ever uses it. I know Eric would use it if he was still here. In fact, we would probably fight over who got to use it. This time I smile at the thought of my little brother and I arguing. I don't see my mother hanging there, but why then, do I have to wipe away another stupid tear? And who is that screaming?

Julie tried saying that Mommy hung herself there like that so that she could go to be with Daddy. I am pretty sure that was just another one of her lies. Mommy didn't even dress herself anymore. I don't know if she even could have hung herself there like that, even if she wanted to.

I did see her hanging there. I tried to pretend that I didn't, but the picture is burned into my mind. I will never be able to forget what I saw. Her eyes that used to be so blue and beautiful were all bulgy out of her head and her face was all swollen and purple when I found her. Her head was hanging funny to the side until I accidentally touched her foot, then it slumped down even more.

It was me that I had heard screaming. I screamed and screamed for what felt like forever that day, until Johnny came running. I will see Mommy hanging from the rope with her head hanging down like that for the rest of my life. This is just one more reason for me to be afraid of going to sleep. My mother is still hanging in that tree, in my nightmares.

Johnny cut the rope she was hanging from almost right away when he saw her, to get her back down on the ground. He said there was no saving her though, her neck was broken and her body was already cold. She must have been hanging there most of the night. Poor Mommy.

I think about hanging myself in the tree that way too. I think about it all the time. I want to be with Mommy,

Daddy, and Eric. I want the hurt to go away and never come back. The only reason that I haven't done it yet is because I still hang on to a little bit of hope that everything will change and get better. The older I get, the more I realize that things will never get better. So far things have only seemed to get worse.

I'm twelve years old now. I'll be thirteen in September. It's been four long years since Eric died and in the fall it will be four years since Daddy died. Mommy died in the summer a whole three years ago now. Julie's baby died around this time too.

Johnny said that the baby wasn't right, that his body was all deranged. I had to ask him what the word deranged meant and he explained that the baby's body wasn't made right, probably because he was an inbred baby. Johnny had to explain what the word inbred meant to me too.

Johnny told me that Daddy was probably Emily's baby's daddy too. Because he was Emily's daddy and her baby's daddy, it made the baby come out all screwed up, all deranged. Johnny said he only lived for a couple of days. I never saw him. Julie wouldn't let me.

I thought about that word, deranged, after Johnny explained what it meant to me. It seems to me that all of us Fleischer's could be described as just a little bit deranged. We are all at least a little screwed up, some of us being more messed up than others.

Julie makes me do most of the girl chores now, all by myself. The only thing she does anymore is the cooking and sometimes I have to do that too, on top of everything else. I do all the laundry, the dishes and cleaning the house. I never cared much for doing the housework and I like it even less now that nobody helps me with it.

I still do a little bit of school work too, just enough to keep anyone from coming around and asking any questions. That's all Julie ever talks about when she makes me do my school work, is keeping the other people from coming in and separating all of us. I don't see why she cares. I'm the only one that's still young enough to be stuck anywhere else for long.

I secretly wish someone would come and take me away. But then it occurs to me that things could be even worse out there, wherever "out there" is. Life has been very hard here in my small little world, but it is the only world that I really know. We are handling things very well for ourselves now without Mommy or Daddy to help, even though I am miserable.

Johnny keeps up with the animals and the vegetables and stuff that we grow. We still sell stuff out at our produce stand by the road in the summer and fall. We don't make a lot of money, but we make some. Johnny doesn't have much time left for anything else by the time he gets done with all his chores.

I don't have much time to do anything besides my chores either, really. I have nothing better than cleaning to do anyways, except think. Thinking doesn't lead my mind anywhere good anymore. When I think, I remember, and I'm so tired of remembering.

I take one last, deep breath of the crisp, clean air, then I head back into the gloomy house to get to work on all the chores that I still have left to start and finish. I will probably have to do some extra laundry today too since it is so nice out.

I have been thinking about testing out the story that Julie told me about leaving the clothes on the line too long. I want to see if Daddy's, Mommy's, or Eric's ghost will really come just to put the clothes on and be able to hang around for a while. If it works, I think I might start leaving the clothes out on the line all the time. I'd like to see my parents and my brother again, even if it's only their spirits that I see.

I want to get some stuff together for that time capsule I plan to bury too. All I can think to put in there is stuff to show who my family is and who I am. There's those newspaper clippings that Emily had found that I could put in there.

Maybe someday someone will find my time capsule and then they will understand some of what our family went through. They might not understand it all, but at least someone else would know. The idea of someone else knowing at least some of the hard times that we have had to go through is a very comforting thought.

I think I'll bury my time capsule out by the willow tree, right under where I found Mommy hanging. Maybe I'll even plant some flowers on top of where I bury it, like I planted the flowers that are now on top of Eric's and Mommy's graves. I still have some of the flower seeds left, and I know that neither Johnny or Julie will use them for anything. The flowers will be far enough away from the swing too so that they won't get trampled by anyone's feet. That's exactly what I'll do.

CHAPTER TWO
Julie

So now things are different and as they should be. I'm in charge and I like it that way. Emily had a really hard time dealing with the feelings that crept up after killing her father and serving him to the family for dinner.

The baby being born all screwed up didn't help her fragile mind any either. For that, I convinced Emily to let me take care of the problem. That kid would have caused nothing but trouble and heartache, if he even managed to live.

Emily and I both almost died giving birth to the little bastard. Johnny helped deliver the baby, but neither one of them could seem to figure out how to get her bleeding to stop afterwards. The bleeding finally slowed down after Emily pushed out a large, bloody mass. I have no idea if that was supposed to be another baby or what, but it was gross.

After Emily's baby was born, he did nothing but cry. Emily couldn't get him to breastfeed and he wouldn't even take a bottle of home-made milk, like what the Fleischer's used to give the runts of the litters of their animals. Emily held and cuddled her baby constantly for two days, often crying right along with the baby out of frustration because she had no idea how to help him.

Two long days after he was born, when Emily finally agreed to let me handle the baby problem, I simply held a pillow over his mixed up little face until a little while after he stopped moving. She wouldn't take him out of the room though, until he really started to stink the place up. She was way too soft.

We both, Emily and I, decided to keep the cradle in the room after burying her freak of a little baby boy in the backyard. I felt like the cradle made an appropriate sleeping place for the doll that Emily once called Julie. I don't need to sleep with a doll and I'm certainly not afraid of her at all, the way that Emily was afraid of me. The doll's name is no longer Julie either. I call her Emily, when I bother to call her anything at all. Only nutcases sit around talking to baby dolls.

Then, with her mother being the useless mess that

she was after she saw us kill her brother-husband and needing to be gotten rid of; well, Emily gave in and finally let me take over for her long-term. I don't plan on letting Emily have the control over us again anytime soon. She would have no idea how to handle things.

It has been hard to run a household with hardly any money, especially during the long winter months. Luckily Emily's father had at least prepared Johnny to be able to handle things, just in case something were to happen to him.

Their father had showed Johnny where all the bills came from, where he kept them, and how to pay them. Johnny had the same name as their father too, except for the Junior at the end, so he wasn't breaking any laws whenever he had to sign his father's name. Most things their father paid for in cash and in person, but for the other stuff, John Sr. had a bank account that he wrote checks from.

At least their father had been nutso about wanting the kids to be able to stay together if anything did happen to him. Over the years, he had carefully trained Johnny in everything he would need to know, just in case. Thankfully, he had also taught Johnny everything he would need to say if anyone official looking came snooping around.

That training had come in handy when a well-dressed, perfectly primped brunette from Child Welfare had come to the front door one day. She said her name was Agnes. One of the bill collectors had gotten suspicious when he hadn't seen their father in over a year and had placed a call to the agency.

Johnny told the snobby lady that his Dad was working out of town and that he sent money home each month for Johnny to pay the bills with. He told her that their father stopped by to check on them every now and then, but for the most part he trusted Johnny to take care of matters because Johnny was old enough to handle things on his own now. Johnny is twenty years old now, after all. He also told the lady that their mother was in and out all the time running errands and such and was normally always home in time to get Caroline to bed.

After a quick peek around the house and in the kitchen cupboards, the stuffy lady named Agnes seemed satisfied. She wished us all well as she left, leaving her business card behind, just in case we might need her at any time in the future. I burned her card in the kitchen sink before her fancy new car was even all the way out of our driveway.

I made Johnny teach me how to drive the truck right after Emily was finally out of the picture. I needed to be able to get around on my own without having to always depend on Johnny and I hated waiting for him to be able to take me where I needed to go.

I have been looking for a real job outside the house in order to be able to keep up with paying the bills. Only selling our left over produce to make money just isn't cutting it any more.

I even bought myself some make-up one day and asked the painted up old lady at the counter to show me how to put it on the right way. The store wasn't busy and she seemed more than willing to give me her experienced advice. She even made me go back and switch a few of the colors I had picked, telling me that these other colors would make my eyes stand out better and such. When she was done showing me how to put the make-up on, I looked in a mirror and realized just how right she was. I looked absolutely drop dead gorgeous!

During my trips alone into town, I have found that it is so easy to get people to do what I want. I have to play it off differently, depending on what I want and who I need to get to help me, but that stuff's not hard now that I have figured it all out.

Take men, for instance; I notice that most of them seem to like my body. They look me up and down with those naughty eyes that say they want to do dirty, nasty things to me. One creep actually had the nerve to offer me money in exchange for a blow job.

First I had made sure that no one else had been listening to our conversation and then I did let him think that I would do exactly what he wanted and maybe even more. He brought me right to his filthy little efficiency apartment. I followed him with my truck, so that we could have some privacy and nobody would know that I had gone with him. Nobody had been around when he made his offer and I made sure that no one saw me go into his apartment either.

The awful stink of his place attacked my nose the minute he opened the only door to his tiny apartment. The sink was piled high with dirty dishes and old, moldy food. There was an open cot sitting in one corner of the apartment with no sheets to cover the stained mattress or pillow. He could have at least covered the ugly mattress with the green blanket that had been shoved to the bottom of the cot. The man's dirty clothes lay strewn all around the edge of the bed, as if even keeping those in a neat pile would have been too much of a strain for him.

I couldn't see clearly into the bathroom, but I could just imagine what that must have looked like by the awful smell that oozed its way out. What a nasty slob.

I'm sure he regretted his offer of money in exchange for a blow job as soon as he felt my teeth crunch down deep into his hardened flesh. He didn't know that I had also been carrying a knife with me and had it waiting in my hand for just the right moment.

When I bit into his throbbing man part I also swung my arm up and used the knife to slice the pig of a man's throat wide open. He had no time to even think about fighting back. He was too busy trying to hold in the blood that was squirting from the gaping wound below his double chin.

Afterwards, I cleaned the man's splattered blood off from my face and other exposed skin in his kitchen sink. I didn't want to step foot in his bathroom. He thought I had taken my clothes off for a completely different reason altogether, but all along it was only so that I wouldn't get his blood on them.

I didn't forget the important part of this whole adventure either, my well-earned pay. I picked up the dark green work trousers that were laying in a heap where he had thrown them only moments before on his grimy floor. Then I took out his worn wallet, peaking quickly at the name on the I.D. card before I helped myself to all the money Mr. Stanley Newburg had in it, forty-three dollars. I shoved the crumpled bills into the pocket of my jean shorts. Not a bad day's work at all. I still can't help but laugh when I think about that day.

Last summer I actually met a guy that I thought I might enjoy getting to know better. He was in town with his family to work at the Fair. That's what his family does. They travel from place to place and earn their living as freaks, on display in their own Freak Show tent. Emily's son would have made a perfect addition as one of their displays, if I hadn't already put him out of his misery and buried him in the backyard. What a shame.

Rufus (the guy I met last summer) considers himself a freak like the rest of the family, but he doesn't look like one at all. He's quite a gentleman too. We spent a lot of time together during the few weeks that he was here last summer. A lot of it we spent in his camper just getting to know each other better. Mostly we did a lot of talking while we smoked some stuff that seemed to make all of life's problems melt away. It made me really hungry too, for some reason. Rufus called the hunger after smoking "having the munchies".

Rufus wanted me to go with him and his family when they left for the next town in September. I wanted to, but there hadn't been enough time to get things ready for me to leave. As much as I wanted to go and leave Emily's life behind to really start my own, I hadn't been ready. Rufus swore he would wait for me and that the offer would still be good this year if I was ready to take it. I'm thinking I will, if he was serious and still wants me when he comes back.

I'm not just some sappy little girl who wants a man to love and take care of her. That type of girl annoys me. That sounds more like what Emily's sister Caroline will be like when she's older.

Rufus is different. He really gets me. I haven't even had sex with him yet and he was ready to give me the world if I would let him. I have not told him all of the Fleischer's deep, dark secrets. I only told him just enough so that he had understood that I wasn't some spoiled girl from a perfect family.

Rufus knows that Emily's dad liked to touch her and that he ended up running off with another woman after the death of her younger brother Eric. He also knows that Emily's mom hung herself in the tree in their backyard after that. Rufus knows that I choose to go by the name Julie now but that I was always Emily until Emily's parents died.

I remember Rufus' touch. It was so gentle. It felt almost like the whisper of a promise of the great things to come. His touch also sent a strange warmth and tingles to the last place that I ever thought I would want to feel anything from ever again, after the horrible things that I had experienced through Emily.

I learned a lot about Rufus during our short time together as well. He had been treated a lot like Emily had during her childhood. He had gone through a lot of beatings just because he looked normal compared to the rest of his family.

Rufus said that the people in his family were mostly all freaks because of all of the inbreeding that had gone on in his family over the years. I haven't met any of the rest of his family yet and I have to admit that I'm a little nervous about it because of everything that I've heard from Rufus.

Rufus' mother and father weren't related to each other like most of the rest of his family were. His grandfather had called his mother a whore for that. She fell in love, actually while working the New York State Fair, and planned to run away with Rufus' father and start a normal life of her own. Her father had found out.

So one day the whole family trapped Rufus' father and beat him almost to death right in front of his mother. Because of that, Rufus' father had fled and never tried to contact his mother again after that. He never even knew Rufus existed that any of them knew of.

Rufus told me how his mother had told him stories as he grew up about the life that they could have had instead of the one that they did. There was such a look of anger and then sadness on his face when he told me that story.

Maybe I could help Rufus locate his father, somehow. Then his mother and father could finally have the life together that she'd always imagined. Maybe, if things worked out like I pictured they would in my head. Right now the only thing I really know is that his name is John.

In only a couple of weeks it will be time for the State Fair again. It seems like it's still so far away. I have been waiting to see if Rufus will be back and if he really still wants me. I feel a little pathetic for being so anxious about seeing him again, but I think Rufus and I will make an amazing team together. No one will be able to hurt either one of us ever again.

This year if he comes and still wants me to go with him, I definitely will. I am planning to bring Caroline with me when I go, even though I can't stand her. She is Emily's little sister, and therefore, kind of my responsibility for now. I certainly can't leave her behind with Johnny, who knows what would happen then. Though, I could try to talk Johnny into coming along to work with Rufus' family as well. We could sell the Fleischer property and split the money. We'll see. Nothing is certain yet.

I'm pretty sure that Johnny has started doing some

of the nasty things to Caroline that their father used to do. I sometimes hear him sneak out of his room at night and I have caught him trying to be alone with her during odd times of the day more than once, though not lately. All I can think is that he must be desperate if he's willing to settle for her. She's fat, doesn't take care of herself, and all she ever does is cry and whine.

I'm pretty sure that even Johnny is getting sick of waking up almost every night to Caroline's blood curdling screams. I hear them from my room all the way upstairs. I've actually gone down to try to shut her up a couple of times.

Caroline keeps having these stupid nightmares where she finds her mother chopped up in little pieces in a plastic bag along the side of her bed. Her mother hung herself, she wasn't cut up! I should know. I helped her with that, a little. Stupid Caroline and her stupid dreams! I really do hate her.

I wouldn't have thought that Johnny would turn out to be just like his father. That kind of surprised me. I know he kissed Emily before their father died, but I had thought that was just because of confused feelings about the things their father had made them do. I also know that Johnny and Emily had a really close relationship as the oldest brother and sister. I guess you just never can tell about some people.

Oh well, now that I have my make-up done and my hair perfectly in place on my head, it's time to get my pretty ass back out in the world to try to find some sort of a job until Rufus comes back, or in case he doesn't come back at all. I know he will be back though, I can feel it. Then everything will be better, I'm sure of it.

CHAPTER THREE
Caroline

Johnny was up and gone before I went out in the kitchen to eat my breakfast and Julie was busy doing whatever it is that she does up in mine and Emily's old bedroom. I only know that because I could hear her walking around and talking to herself while I heated up some of the rice that we had with dinner last night.

Hot rice with milk and honey is really good. Plus, there were no eggs or anything ready this morning, so I figured it should be okay if I helped myself to something else.

My thoughts are interrupted when I hear the engine of Daddy's old truck start. Julie must be taking off to somewhere again. She's always doing that lately.

I wish that I could just get in the truck and take off whenever I wanted to. I'm not sure where I would go or what I would do when I left, but just to know that I could would be nice, I think.

Julie hollers my name out. Oh no! What does she want to yell at me for this time? I hurry to get off the swing and run as fast as I can through the overgrown lawn around the house to the driveway. When I get close enough, I can see that she's laughing and shaking her head at me. My heart is racing from running and worrying and I'm all out of breath.

"You're such a fatty," she yells to me in between her fits of laughter, that I know are at my cost. She gets out of the rusty old truck as I get close enough to her for her to do whatever yelling at me she needs to do before she leaves. She grabs me by the back of my hair, twisting it painfully tight so that she has a good hold with her fist, and then pulls my face to hers. Her breath smells minty. She either just brushed recently or she's chewing gum. I'd like some gum to chew.

"I know what your nasty slob ass is trying to do with Johnny. That's gross and you need to keep him away from you or you'll end up with another baby that none of us wants or can afford to take care of." I have to avoid wiping away the spit that landed on my face while Julie was screaming at me. That would set her off on another tantrum for sure.

Tears of pain start to escape from my eyes. "No Julie, I don't want that." Shamefully I add, "Johnny doesn't want me like that anyways." She roughly lets go of my hair, pulling some of the strands right out with her fingers as she shoves me to the sharp rocks in the dirt driveway again, just like she always does.

"Good. Now don't get lazy and forget about doing your chores today."

I manage to whisper from my spot on the ground, "I won't," in response before she carries on some more.

"I would stay and do them myself to make sure they get done right, but one of us has to suck it up and look for a real job in order to pay all these bills. This selling crops sure isn't cutting it. Do the chores before you go off and play anymore, so you don't forget. Now get out of my face. I can barely stand to look at you with that snot dripping down from your fat nose, you nasty, fat, little pig!"

I pick myself up off the stony dirt and head quickly to the house before Julie can figure out something else to yell at me for. With a sad little sniffle and a sigh of relief, I enter the house and close the door behind me. Just as it closes completely, I hear the truck's engine fade into the distance as it moves away from our house and down the road towards town.

I walk through the gloomy living room into the slightly brighter kitchen. The smells from breakfast are still strong enough to be able to tell what we each ate. I have always thought that the smell of food is comforting. The feeling of comfort quickly fades when I see the small pile of dirty dishes that are still waiting for my attention.

I'm still too tired to start washing the dishes yet. So I push my fat self out the screen door to go sit back on my swing for just a little while longer. I just need a little more time before I start on all the never ending work that is waiting for me in the house. I know in my head that this is stupid of me. I know that I should just start the work and get it over with as quick as I can, but I just don't feel like doing any of it. I'm sure that I will be able to get it all done long before Julie gets back home.

I hear high-pitched chirping from what must be baby birds because it is a sharper chirp than a grown bird would make. Then I see an adult blackbird fly over me and I follow it with my eyes. It lands in a nest up in the willow tree, the same tree my swing is hanging from, the same tree my mother's dead body hung from. I watch as closely as I can while the baby birds chirp and the mommy or daddy bird feeds them. It seems a little late in the summer for baby birds. I guess the birds must be as confused and lost as I feel.

Watching the birds care for each other makes me sad all over again. I feel so alone with no one to really take care of me or love me the way that I know my mommy and daddy did. Why did things have to happen this way? Why was I left all by myself here with only Johnny to really care about what happens to me? Why did they all leave me? Why did they all have to die without me?

Johnny's a little strange though. I mean, he confuses me. He has come into my room at night and started to show me love the way that Daddy did sometimes, but then he gets mad before he really starts anything and just stops and leaves. He always says he's sorry too.

Daddy told me it's only natural, what he used to do, and that he only did it because he really loved me and thought that I was special. Maybe Johnny is trying really hard to make me feel loved and special, but he just doesn't really feel that way. It makes me feel very bad when he gets mad like that and leaves. Maybe I am doing something wrong or maybe no one else will be able to love me in the special way that Daddy did ever again.

Johnny hasn't bothered coming around like that any time lately though, so I don't know why Julie was yelling at me about it today. Sometimes I just think that she makes up excuses to shout at me.

I decide to get down off the swing and walk over to the spot in the garden where Eric is buried. There are beautiful flowers growing all around his grave now. I planted them myself in the early spring. His grave. Where my little brother Eric's dead body is rotting in the dirt below the ground.

I'm crying now and I fall to my knees next to the spot where I know Eric's body is. I know in my head that his spirit isn't really with his body anymore, but I like to think that at least a part of him is here with me. "Eric, everything is all screwed up now. Nothing has been right ever since you left us. I wish you were here still and that everything would be like it was before you died. I miss you so much."

I lie on the ground next to Eric's grave. Somehow I find that I am comfortable. The raw smell of the earth fills my nose. It almost reminds me of the way my father's hands smelled, except here I can also smell the mixed scents of the flowers. It feels like someone has picked me up in their huge arms and is holding me tightly to make me feel better. Strangely enough, I do feel a calming sense that everything is going to be alright wash over me. I let myself drift off into a sweet, peaceful sleep right on the ground where I am lying.

I'm not sure how long I slept for, but I wake up feeling much better than I did before I fell asleep. I wipe the grass and dirt from my face as I sit up slowly, looking around me. The sun is still shining and, except for the sounds of the animals and insects, everything is still as peaceful and quiet as when I first lay my head down.

I need to use the bathroom, but I hate the idea of going back inside that big, empty house all alone. I'll throw some laundry in the wash so I at least have an excuse to come back out later to hang the clothes on the line to dry. So I make my way slowly back into the gloomy house. I note on my way through the kitchen that, of course, the dirty dishes haven't been washed by anyone else while I was napping.

I also notice the time. It's already two o'clock! I should have started making something for supper long before now. Julie told me before that if she doesn't start something for that night's supper by noon, then I need to make sure to figure something out.

I need to get those dishes washed too before Julie gets home. There's so much to do and I still don't feel like doing any of it. I don't understand the point of it any more. I don't really understand the point of anything anymore.

Well, I know one thing, if I don't start getting busy fast,

Julie's going to try to make me understand one good reason for getting things done around here. I don't want to have to deal with her, so right after I go potty, I'll get started.

I'll make a tossed salad to go with our supper for tonight. That's pretty quick and easy. Plus, picking the vegetables I'll need will give me another good reason to spend some time outside. Now I just have to figure out what to make to eat with the salad.

First I'll throw a load of wash in to get started. The basket from the bathroom is so heavy, it's hard to carry down the basement stairs. I can barely lift it off the ground and I have to set the basket down at each stair. I worry that one of these times I'll fall down the stairs and hurt myself when I'm lugging the basket. Nobody would probably find me for a long time and I would die slowly and painfully all by myself with the rats crawling over me.

We used to keep most of our dirty laundry all separate, but now that there are only the three of us it's just easier to keep it all in one place and wash it when the basket fills up. This way everyone's laundry gets washed without worrying about who needs laundry done and who doesn't. I still have to strip the bedding off from each of our beds every now and then to wash that too, but that doesn't get washed and changed half as much anymore as when Mommy and Daddy were still around.

The basement smells so old and dirty. I don't like coming down here at all. I really hate coming down here by myself especially. I can't imagine how poor Emily must have felt when she had to sleep down here. I can hear the rodents running around in the dark corners. I throw the dirty clothes in the washer as fast as I can and then add the soap. Then I run up the stairs, back to a less creepy part of the house.

I can gather the vegetables that I'll need for the salad after I hang the clothes out to dry later. Then I remember that there is still some chicken in the refrigerator that Julie decided not to make for last night's dinner. At least it's not frozen and it can just be thrown right into a pan and put in the oven.

I wonder where Julie took off to when she left or where Johnny has been all day. It would be nice if even just once in a while one of them would ask me to go along with them for a change. I really don't like to be stuck here all alone, especially with all these chores to do.

It seemed like the chores would go by so fast when the whole family worked on them together. Maybe it was just having someone to keep me company that made them feel like they got done more quickly than they do here lately. It doesn't matter now, I guess. Now I do all the girly, boring chores all by myself.

I should wash the few dirty dishes that are in the sink while the clothes are washing so that they are done before Julie comes back. I know that there are only a few, but they seem to be filling the whole sink. I hate washing the dishes. I liked rinsing them after Emily washed them, but I don't like having to scrub and wash them all by myself. Rinsing was so much easier than washing is.

Through the screen door I can see that the sky looks like it is getting darker. I should really go pick the few vegetables I will need to make the salad now, just in case it decides to rain. I grab our big white bowl from the cupboard next to the refrigerator to gather the vegetables in. Then I head outside.

The wind is blowing my hair around so that I have to keep brushing it out of my eyes with my hand, but the dark clouds are still a little ways away. I realize now that I should have pulled my hair back with a rubber band. It probably will rain a little later on, I would bet money on that... if I had any. I guess I will have to hang the clothes inside the house to dry when it's time.

I walk with the bowl that I took from the house over to the part of the garden where the vegetables are planted. Carefully, I take my time to find the biggest head of lettuce, the healthiest bunch of carrots, the ripest looking cucumber, a nice big red tomato, and some decent sized radishes. At least if I can prepare a decent meal it will make me feel like my life is worth a little something.

Then I decide to take a break for just a few minutes on my swing before heading back into the house with my bowl full of fresh vegetables. It took me quite a while to gather those vegetables and it's more tiring work than it seems like it would be. I think that I deserve a little bit of a break. I'm not sitting on the swing long at all before I hear a familiar sound and then see the object that is making that sound.

There's a truck making its way down the driveway. The dust clouds that the truck made on its way through are still settling back in to the dirt. That's not just the sound of any old truck either. It's Daddy's. There's a horrible ear piercing squealing coming from the engine now that gives it away every time. It has been making that sound for about a month now.

My heart starts to beat faster, wondering what Julie will do to me because I haven't gotten everything finished that I was supposed to yet.

ING

CHAPTER FOUR
Julie

Life is finally okay for a change. I'm cruising down the road in Emily's dead father's old pickup and 'I Will Survive' comes blaring out of the radio on the dashboard. I turn the knob so the music now drowns out even the sound of my own voice as I sing along. I think this song fits me so well. Of course I will survive. I think I've proven to myself that I can handle just about anything that gets thrown my way.

First I decide to stop in at the diner. I've never been in here before and neither has Emily, even though she only lived about twenty minutes away from it for her whole life. It's a cute little place full of greasy, delicious smelling air and even greasier men. No matter, the men can be easily overlooked.

The waitress that's working is an older woman than me, probably about the age Emily's mother would be if she were still alive. She looks really tired and stressed out. There are bags under her eyes and every inch of skin that I can see is sagging.

I start to slowly approach the counter where the cash register is, avoiding the grabby hands as best as I can on my way past. Why are all men like that? What makes them think that they have the right to just grab any stranger in any way that they want to? Are there actually girls and women around that put up with that sort of behavior, or worse yet, even like it?

There's an old fat man impatiently waiting on the other side of the register for me to say what it is I am here for. He has an apron on that is supposed to be white, but is filthy with grease and remnants of other food. I can already tell I'm not going to get along with him.

Just as I open my mouth to speak, a tray full of food is almost thrown at an opening between the back of the diner and the front. The old fat man turns around to look behind him and then shouts, "order up," to the tired looking waitress who is taking an order from a group of three snobby looking teenage girls.

Each of the three girls look like they come from rich families with clothes that look like they came straight out of a magazine, fancy purses, and perfectly primped hair. I immediately hate them.

"Now what can I help you with, Miss," the fat man's second chin wiggles as he snaps impatiently at me. He doesn't look at my face when he speaks to me, but up and down the length of my body instead. It feels as if he is sizing me up, deciding if my body is worth any of his precious time.

"I was wondering if you are looking for any help here," I say, looking to my side as the sound of shattering dishes on the dirty diner floor makes me jump.

The fat man slams his fist on the counter and yells at the worn out, middle aged waitress, "Damn it Bev! You're costing me more money than you are worth! Clean your mess and get back to work. I'm taking this out of your pay this week."

The waitress looks back down at the shattered pieces of dishes mixed with leftover food and continues to clean up the mess. She must really need the money to put up with working in a place like this. I want to yell at him and tell him to cut the poor lady some slack, but it's not my place and I need a job too. She must be used to being treated poorly anyhow, the way that she barely reacted when he yelled at her like that.

He turns his nothing but negative attention back to me. This doesn't seem like such a cute little diner now and I'm not feeling so good about working here anymore. Actually, the thought occurs to me that I should chop this fat pig into tiny little pieces, keeping him alive as long as I can while I do it, just so that I can hear him squeal out in pain.

"Unless you want to suck my cock, I don't have the time or the patience to train someone new that has no experience."

This rude, nasty statement brings a round of chuckles from the greasy men sitting around the counter and a dirty look from the obviously experienced waitress who is still cleaning up the remains of broken plates and cups from the floor.

Then the jerk has the nerve to add, "Now unless you're going to buy something to eat or drink, quit wasting my time and get the hell out of my diner."

I feel my face grow hot with anger. I'm not embarrassed. This fat piece of shit couldn't say anything *that would make me blush out of embarrassment. I can't think of anything fitting to say, so I flip everyone in the slimy diner the bird as I turn on my heel and walk out the door.*

Of course, right after I leave several ideas for what I could have and should have said fill my mind, but it's too late. There is no way I'll go back in that ratty place ever again.

I hop back up in my beat up, rusty, old pickup (yes, I consider it mine now) and slam the door shut behind me as hard as I can. I rev the truck's engine and peel out of the diner's parking lot, not sure where exactly I want to head next.

I should be grateful that I didn't get a job offer at that seedy little diner. I was only in there for less than ten minutes and I still feel slimy from the layer of grease that I can feel almost slithering over my skin.

'Jessie's Girl' starts playing on the car radio. I crank it up and look out the truck's dusty windshield, trying to figure out where I should make my next stop. I've gotten pretty much the same response everywhere that I have gone so far.

Nobody wants a young girl with no experience, not in this town anyhow. If any one of them would only give me half a chance, they would see that I can do just about anything that I put my mind to, and that I'm not just a pretty face.

I turn the truck around, deciding to completely head out of Dereves in my search for a job. There are plenty of diners and other small stores of all sorts in the city of Syracuse. One of them will be sure to hire me. I have to pass the Fairgrounds on the way, so I might as well peek to see if any of the workers have started setting up camp for this year's fair yet.

It doesn't take me long to get to the road that the Fair is on, probably only about half an hour. I want Rufus to be there, but at the same time I kind of hope that he's not. I really feel like I need a good bath to scrub myself clean after my latest job hunting adventure. Maybe I should just head back home and forget my search for today.

No, I can't let any doubt edge its way into my thoughts. Then I would be just like Emily, always worried about saying and doing the right thing. Screw that.

My heart flutters when I see several campers sitting in the parking lot on the grounds to the Fair. Should I park so that I can get out and take a closer look to see if Rufus might be here yet? If he is here, will he think I'm acting too desperate and not want anything to do with me?

Stop it right now Julie. Park this beast and take your sexy ass to find your man. You know he'll want you. Who doesn't? This is my own voice inside my head, trying to talk some sense into myself. It's not like when I would talk to Emily, there's no room for anyone else in this body. This body is mine now and Emily is just somewhere deep inside, hiding from the world like the chicken that she is. I'm in control now and I think I am doing a damn good job.

I put the truck in park, take a deep breath, and open the door. I jump down from the torn seat cushion, careful not to get the spring caught in my shorts. I'll head towards the campers first, to see if the one Rufus drives is even here yet.

Before I even have a chance to get close to any of the campers, I hear a familiar, deep voice call my name.

"Julie, is that you?" The voice speaks again. My heart does a somersault in my chest. That's his voice. I turn to look in the direction of the buildings and see Rufus quickly heading my way. I stay put, waiting for him to reach me.

"Julie, I'm so happy to see you. How did you know I would be here today," he asks as he wraps me up tight in

his arms.

My head is buried in his chest now and I breathe his scent in as deeply as I can before pulling my head back to answer him. "I didn't know if you would be here yet or not, but I was hoping like hell that you were."

We go back to Rufus' camper and quickly catch up on everything that's happened over the last year with each other while we share a joint. That's what Rufus calls it. He thinks it's funny how I'm so naïve about this stuff. Naïve or not, this stuff makes me feel good, slow and good. I'm glad that Rufus has been showing me some of his ways, especially where this stuff is concerned.

I tell him all about what happened at the diner, even what the overweight bastard said to me just before I walked out. When I am all finished with my crappy story about what happened, Rufus' face is twisted up in anger as he says, "We'll show them all. Come on."

He grabs a large gas can from the front of the camper and then motions me to follow him back outside.

"Come on, we'll take your truck. My family doesn't need my help to set up any more today anyways," he says, waving his hand toward the fairgrounds.

Rufus pushes the driver's seat of the truck back to fit his taller body frame. I hop in the passenger's side next to him and we pull out of the parking lot of the State Fair.

"Where is this diner you were telling me about," he wants to know.

So I give him the directions, curious about what he has planned. I don't have to wait long at all for an answer to the question that I never asked out loud.

"When we get there I want you to take that can and spread the gas out as much as you can all around the place. Then get back in the truck. Wait for me to give you the okay before you get out of the truck though. We don't want to get caught."

His front teeth are falling apart. I think that only adds to his rough, sexy look. I wonder if they hurt. I've had toothaches a few times, and they hurt like hell, if you ask me.

I'm not nervous about this plan Rufus has. Actually, I'm a little excited and feeling kind of tingly down below thinking that he is actually going to do something so big just because the jerks inside were rude to me. Then, in a quick flash of guilt, I remember the tired looking, middle aged waitress.

"Wait Rufus. There's a waitress there that..." He cuts me off with a stern look that I've never seen from *him before.*

"Hey Beautiful, we can't risk anyone at all seeing us. And do you think that waitress is gonna just sit back and watch while we burn that horrible place down and do nothing?"

He's right. He is older than me by a few years, so of course he knows more. Plus, he's been around tons of other people and travelled the country his whole life.

Emily only ever had quick conversations with strangers that stopped at the produce stand here and there. And to be honest with myself, I really have no clue what kind of a person that waitress is anyways. Maybe she's a horrible person. It's probably best for me not to think about it too much.

I look out the window on my side of the truck and realize that we're getting very close to the diner now. "Yeah, you're right. The bitch probably deserves it even more than those nasty pigs do," I say as I turn back to look at him.

Most of the people that had been there when I stopped in were probably gone by now anyhow. I secretly hope that by some chance those three spoiled teenage bitches are in there when the place goes up in flames.

When we get to the full parking lot of the diner, Rufus looks out the windshield slowly, from one side to the other. "Do you see anyone," he asks me in a whisper, as if someone we can't see might hear him. The lunch crowd must be here now.

"Nope, all clear. Want me to go spread the gas now?" I have my hand on the door handle, ready with nervous energy to do this and get it over with.

He looks me straight in the eyes and says, "Yes, but be careful. Try to hide quick if you see anyone at all."

He kisses me long and hard on my mouth, giving me butterflies in my stomach before taking one more quick look around outside the truck. Then we both get out of the truck, me with the gas can. He has a two by four, a hammer, and nails with him. As I'm pouring the gas around as fast as I can, I'm watching the man that I think I might be falling madly in love with.

Rufus is nailing the board to the door so that all the people inside will be trapped once the fire is started. I wonder if any of them even hear the hammering against the door. I sure can hear it. I'm not sure how anyone inside could miss it.

Strangely, I find that I love the smell of the gas that I'm pouring and it's making me feel a little light-headed.

I splash the last of it against the tin box that the diner calls home. Then I take a quick look around to make sure no one is watching before running back to the safety of my rusty old truck.

I watch Rufus as he backs himself away from the entrance to the diner. He pulls something from the pocket of his jeans. I'm not sure what it is until I see the small flame after he strikes it. I watch him throw the lit match towards the diner before he runs quickly back to the truck where I'm waiting anxiously for him.

The fire catches quickly, flaring up and creating a thick black smoke that seems to almost be sending a cry for help up into the clear blue sky. I didn't notice all the faces in the windows of the diner until now. I'm not sure how I managed to miss them before.

Just before we peel out of the parking lot I see the face of the waitress from earlier appear in one of the windows, a look of pure terror now replacing the tired look on her face.

I swear I can hear the many people from inside the diner screaming now. I can smell them burning too. The air had smelled of greasy fried food and now it smells like burning human flesh. It's a smell like no other and one that I don't think that I'll ever forget. I had smelled that same smell when Emily's father branded all of their asses.

There's actually an acidy taste in my mouth because I feel so bad about what I just did. I turn the radio up loud, to drown out any possible noise that might come from the burning diner. I don't really hear the music, but it's nice not to be able to hear anything else for a few minutes too, at least until we can put some distance between us and the diner.

I don't need to feel bad. All of those people deserved what they got. I'm sure that every single one of them had something that they deserved to be burned alive for. Well, Emily was always told that the smoke from a fire would kill people long before the actual fire could burn them. Besides, I'm sure the fire department will be there soon to put out the flames and everyone will be just fine.

After we drive with only the sound of the radio for a few miles, Rufus turns the radio off and turns to look at me. "You okay, Beautiful," he asks with concern.

I smile the sweetest smile I can at him and nod. I can still see the black smoke in the sky from the burning diner. "That was so crazy! I can't believe you did that for me." That's what I need to focus on, the fact that Rufus did all of this for me and only me, and not the fact that I haven't heard a single siren from the fire hall go off yet.

He reaches over to take my shaking hand in his strong, steady hand and squeezes it as he says, "I would do anything for you and I won't ever let anyone hurt you again. Now tell me how to get to your house from here. I want to see this place you grew up in and where you spend so much of your time."

I gladly give him the directions to my house, eager to have something else to keep my troubled mind busy for a while. I scoot closer to Rufus so I can lay my head on his muscular arm as we finish our trip to the house that Emily and I grew up in.

CHAPTER FIVE
Caroline

"Caroline! Get your ass in here right now," I hear Julie scream to me from the house, instantly breaking me away from my depressing thoughts. She must not have had any promising job leads during her trip into town today. She's been trying to find a waitressing job to help pay some of the bills. So far she hasn't had any luck.

I try to think quickly about why she would be yelling at me this time and then I suddenly remember. I haven't washed the small pile of dirty dishes from breakfast yet. I'm sure that must be what she's hollering about. That, and the fact that she's probably in a bad mood from yet another wasted day of job hunting.

I jump down from the swing, grabbing my bowl full of vegetables for the salad after I'm back on the ground, to head toward the house and whatever punishment is waiting for me inside this time. When I walk through the screen door I see a strange man standing in the kitchen with Julie. This startles me and I almost drop the bowl of vegetables

I'm carrying.

Luckily, I recover quickly from the shock of seeing an unfamiliar face in our house and go about setting the bowl on the counter. The man looks a little like Daddy and Johnny with short brown hair and a slender build. He's about as tall as Johnny is too, standing about a foot taller than Julie. I'm careful not to look at him for too long.

"Caroline, why are there dirty dishes still sitting on the counter? I bring someone home and this is what I find when I walk in? Get them done now, please."

She's trying to use a nice voice. I can tell because it sounds so fake and I don't think she has ever once used the word please when she was talking to me or even to Johnny. If that man weren't standing here with us right now I know she would be yelling and probably hitting me, like she normally does.

I don't say anything. I just walk over to the sink and start filling it with soap and water. It's better not to say anything at all when Julie is upset. This I figured out the hard way over the past few years. Maybe I'll get off easy today because that man is here with her.

"Aren't you even going to say hello to my boyfriend Rufus, Caroline? He's going to get me a job working the Fair this year. His family works a lot of the fairs and circuses all over the country. He can probably get all of us jobs with his family."

I turn around to face Julie and the guy Rufus that is standing with her. He is smiling at me, but I don't have a good feeling about him. He gives me the creeps.

I quietly say, "Hello, it's nice to meet you, Rufus," to be polite and then turn back to face the dishes that I put in the sink to wash. I don't like Julie and her boyfriend standing there behind me while I have my back to them washing dishes. Just as I'm thinking this, I hear Julie whisper something loudly to Rufus who chuckles, followed by a giggle from Julie, and then they finally leave me alone in the kitchen.

I should have done these stupid dishes hours ago. The rice is stuck to the bowl that I used for rice cereal, there is egg stuck to the frying pan that either Johnny or Julie cooked in, and each of the cups has a ring of milk or juice stuck around the bottom of it. This is my fault. If I had done the dishes right away instead of waiting so long, they would have been a lot easier to wash.

I finally finish scrubbing the dishes, rinsing, drying, and putting them away, and then I decide to look around for Johnny. He must still be outside somewhere, probably feeding the animals or busy doing some other chore. It's quickly getting very dark outside. The sun is now behind the group of dark clouds that I had seen further away in the sky earlier. I can tell it's going to start raining any minute. The air is heavy with that fresh rain smell.

Johnny's not in the field planting seeds or pulling weeds so they don't ruin our crops and he's not out feeding the chickens. I stop for a moment and think of where else he might possibly be. Then I realize he must be milking the cow or tending the horse. But when I go to look, he's not in either of those places. I check around in the barn too, just to be sure he's not doing something in there.

Where else could he be? I walk back out of the barn and stand out in the open grass, just looking around carefully for my older brother. He must be here somewhere. I have not seen him all day and he normally tends the animals for a second time by now.

A feeling of doom washes over me. What if Johnny left and he's gone forever now? I don't want to be stuck here alone with Julie and that guy Rufus. I'm starting to panic and tears are making their way down my chubby cheeks, making my face start to itch. "Johnny," I yell out his name as loud as I can, worried and afraid that I won't get an answer back.

Just then, rain begins to pour down from the sky. A streak of lightening brightens up the strangely dark afternoon sky and a few seconds later I hear a large boom of thunder. I'm crying harder now, but my tears are no match for the heavy rain that is beginning to soak my hair, face, and clothes. It doesn't even occur to me that I should probably go back inside the house to get away from the weather.

Then I think I hear someone shouting at me over the sound of the rain pelting down on the roof of the barn. Johnny is running towards me, his head bent down in an obvious attempt to avoid getting wet with the rain. I can tell he's already soaked through.

He's got his fishing pole in his left hand and his tackle box in his right. That's what he was doing. A huge feeling of relief takes the place of the terror I was feeling only moments before.

"Come on, let's get in the house," Johnny shouts as he reaches me and we run the rest of the way to the house together. Once we are inside and out of the rain, I realize just how drenched I really am. My dripping clothes are clinging to my shivering body.

"Go change out of your wet clothes now before you catch a cold," Johnny orders me as he sets down his fishing gear. He leans his pole against the counter and sets the tackle box on top of the counter.

As I'm heading out of the kitchen and hear a man's rough voice coming from up the stairs, I remember why I was looking for my older brother in the first place. Johnny hears it too, I can tell by the puzzled look on his face.

"Julie brought a man home with her Johnny and she says she's going to work at the Fair with him. She said his name is Rufus and he's her boyfriend." I can see the anger clear as day on Johnny's face.

"Okay, just go get changed. Don't you worry about that," Johnny motions towards the stairs as he speaks. "I'll take care of it." He heads toward the stairs and I go to my bedroom to do as he told me.

I'm not even finished getting my wet clothes off from my shivering body yet when I hear banging and shouting from upstairs. Now I'm worried about Johnny. I try to hurry up with taking my pants off, but rushing seems to make it take even longer. I can't seem to get this stupid pant leg down around my foot. Deciding that I'm too scared to go see what's going on anyways, I slow myself back down so that I can actually get my wet clothes off from myself. I sit on the edge of my bed so that I won't fall over.

Finally, once all my wet clothes are off, I run my towel quickly over my naked body and then rub my hair with the towel to dry it at least enough so that it won't drip anymore. Hopefully I won't have as hard of a time getting dry clothes back on myself as I did taking the wet ones off.

I can still hear shouting and banging around coming from upstairs. I hear Julie yell out a couple of times, but mostly it's Johnny and that other man named Rufus that I hear. I can't make out exactly what they are saying, but I do know that they aren't happy at all with each other.

Once I have some dry clothes on, I grab my hair brush and look at myself in the mirror. I cringe at what I see. I never like the girl that I see looking back at me from the other side of the mirror. She's too fat and has ugly pimples covering her face.

Now my hair looks like a tangled, wet mess too. It's never pretty anymore now that Mommy is gone, but right now it's even worse than normal. I wish I looked more like Julie does and acted more like Emily did before Julie took over. Julie's right, I'm nothing but a fat slob that nobody could possibly want anymore.

CHAPTER SIX
Julie

Rufus definitely has the upper hand in this fight between him and Johnny. Johnny is getting the living crap beat out of him like I haven't seen since their father was alive and he is stupidly still getting back up for more.

All me and Rufus were even doing was making out on my bed when Emily's brother so rudely interrupted. I don't see why Johnny got so bent out of shape about it. He has to be jealous of Rufus, that's all I can think.

Johnny had come up thinking he was going to play Daddy and instead is getting told how things around here are going to be from now on. I really like seeing this side of Rufus. I'm getting those funny warm tingles down below all over again. Rufus lets Johnny know, without a shadow of a doubt, that he is the man in this picture and when he is around, he alone will be the boss.

"Over my dead body," Johnny stands up from the worn hardwood floor again to challenge Rufus.

"Now Johnny Boy, if that's what you really want, I would be happy to help you out. Otherwise, I think you need to start seeing the real picture here, the new picture." Johnny storms out of the bedroom and Rufus follows.

"Stay the hell away from me," Johnny hollers over his shoulder just before Rufus throws him right down the staircase.

Rufus comes back over to where I am standing in the doorway of my bedroom, stands directly in front of me, and puts his arms around my waist. He bends his knees slightly so that he is nose to nose with me as he searches my face for forgiveness or approval, I'm not sure which.

"Baby, I'm so sorry I had to do that. I have to set the boundaries now or he'll think that you're always going to be his property. Do you still love me?" He gives me the most adorable puppy dog eyes and pouts his gorgeous lips, waiting for a reply from me.

"Oh Rufus, of course I still love you, Honey. In fact, I thought that was hot as hell!"

After he shuts the door to my bedroom again, we make out some more, this time Rufus undressing me as we kiss. I don't fuss or complain, I am ready to give myself to him completely. His lips are so soft against mine, his tongue gently feeling around the inside of my mouth. I love the way he tastes like cigarettes, cooked onions, and a light hint of that pot stuff.

Then I feel his kiss become more insistent as he undoes my shorts and pushes them down my legs, along with my panties. Once I'm naked from the waist down, he begins to explore all of the other parts of my body with his hands.

I want him. I want him so badly that I almost forget all about Johnny who was just thrown down the stairs only a couple of minutes ago. I'm sure that he's fine and, even if not, I know Caroline will let me know or take care of his wounds by herself. Honestly, I don't really care if he's okay or not and I hope that Caroline does deal with it so that Rufus and I can spend this time alone together.

After pulling my shirt off over my head, Rufus starts to nibble on my neck, which gives me goose bumps and makes me giggle like a damn little girl would. I irritate myself with the giggling, so I stop him from going after my neck any more by grabbing at the belt of his pants and pulling my head away from his to be able to see what I'm doing better. I guess I'm not fast enough for

Rufus because he takes over and undoes his own pants, letting them drop to the floor and then stepping out of them one foot at a time.

I purposely don't look at his man part. I don't like the way it looks. Well, not his, I don't know what his looks like yet, but any man parts. I just do not like to look at them. It's embarrassing too. I don't think I'm really supposed to make it obvious if I do look anyhow.

I am completely naked. I am pretty sure that by this point Rufus has taken a good, long look at every single part of my body. He walks over to me and places his hands at the back of my head, twining my long hair between his big fingers. Then he lifts my head with his thumbs that are holding under my chin so that I have no choice but to look into his face.

"I love you and I want to marry you, Julie. I want to marry you and start a family of our own with you."

I clear my throat as I feel my face beginning to flush. I'm not quite sure what to say to him in response. This seems so sudden, but not sudden at all at the same exact time.

Of course I want to marry him and start a family with him, or at least I think I do. Don't I? I've been looking forward to seeing him again and to going away with him to work with his family for a whole year now.

"Yes Rufus, let's do it. Let's get married!"

He almost smothers me with his next kiss and I love it. I take his hand and walk him over to my twin bed that suddenly seems much too small for the both of us. As we make our way there, he pauses to trace the "F" that will forever mark my right butt cheek.

Before Rufus can ask me the reason why the "F" is there, I say, "That's a story for another time. All of us in this house have one on our butts." I push what is one of many of Emily's bad memories out of my head and then I lay down on my back and pull Rufus' body down to meet mine.

Rufus begins to kiss me all over, even on my girl part, which tickles and makes me laugh. He licks me there, which sends shivers all the way up to my shoulders. Then he brings his face to mine again as his hardened man part pushes gently at the opening of my moistened girl part.

"We belong with each other," he whispers in my ear just before he nibbles on my neck again and pushes his part between the folds of my own part. Then he slowly pushes himself deeper inside of me. It hurts and stings a little at first, but the pain quickly disappears, leaving me *feeling whole and loved in a way that I have never felt.*

This man that I have fallen so deeply in love with is inside of me. I can hear his breathing and feel the warmth of it on my naked shoulder. We are one at this moment. I want to remember every single minute of our first time together. I have never experienced anything like this in my entire life. This I want. This feels like heaven might feel like, if I actually believed in God.

I'm not sure why, but I begin to cry. Rufus licks the tears from the sides of my face and hugs his body closer to mine as he continues to thrust himself in deeper and then pulls back a little before pushing back in again.

It hurts when he's inside of me as deep as he can go, but I force myself to enjoy the pain. This is a good pain. I feel a strong tingle in my pee area, almost as if a horrible itch is being scratched. Then I scream out as the feeling gets so strong that I just can't help myself.

Rufus' thrusts get stronger and faster until he moans and I feel his warmth rush through my insides as he collapses onto me. After a couple of minutes, he rolls his body off from mine to lay beside me on my bed. We're both breathing heavily and sweating.

"That was great. I gotta go grab my smokes out of the truck, Beautiful. You wanna come with me and just

get out of here for a while or what," he asks as he slides his blue jeans back on over his thin but muscular legs.

"I think I need a little nap," I laugh nervously, thinking about what we just did together. I don't want to keep him from doing something he may need to do though, so I say, "but if you need to go somewhere you can take the truck and just come back for me when you can. Or you can even come back here to spend the night with me."

After he throws his t-shirt back on over his head, he says, "If you don't mind, I should stop back by the fairgrounds to let my family know where I'll be and see if they need any help with anything before I leave for the night. I would just stay, but they would come looking for me and kick both of our asses." He runs his fingers back through his hair to straighten it out. Surprisingly, it goes right back into place and looks gorgeous.

He bends to kiss me sweetly on my forehead and then covers me up with my sheet. Then he says, "I'll be back. Rest up, you're going to need it for when I get back tonight." I bite my lower lip and smile at him. He winks at me as he leaves my bedroom and shuts the door behind him.

I am so sleepy. I can't believe how tired I am. Then I think about everything that has happened during this *day so far. No wonder I'm exhausted. It has been a very long and busy day. I'm still completely naked under my sheet. I don't care. I lay my head back down on my pillow and snuggle myself to get comfortable against the bed.*

As I drift off to sleep, I hear Emily trying to talk to me. Her voice is very faint and weak, but I can still hear it.

"You're moving way too fast, Julie. You don't know that man at all. You're letting your heart make decisions for you, which is not like you at all. Can I please come back? I'll be okay now, I promise. Please let me have my life back?"

What a stupid baby she is. She is no better than Caroline now. She just wants the amazing life that I have finally started making for myself. No way. This is my life now and, right this minute, I need some sleep.

CHAPTER SEVEN
Caroline

I hear a loud crashing and banging. Someone fell down the stairs, I'm sure of it. Should I stay put or go out and see who fell and whether or not they're okay? I don't want to get screamed at, or worse, but I'm worried about Johnny. I don't know what I would do without him. Julie hates me. My older brother is the only one left in the whole world that cares anything about me.

With that thought, I can't hold myself back any longer. Even though my heart feels like it's about to jump right out of my throat, I run out towards the staircase to see what happened.

Johnny is lying on the floor at the bottom of the stairs and his head is bleeding like crazy. "Oh my God! Are you hurt anywhere else, Johnny? What happened?" I kneel down beside him and try to check him over for more bleeding.

"I'm fine Caroline. Just go get me a rag for my head

please." He starts to sit himself up, feeling carefully at the gushing wound on his head with his fingers. His lip is split and bleeding too and it looks as if he might have a black eye.

I get up and go to the kitchen sink to get a rag and wet it like Johnny asked me to. I quickly grab a rag from the drawer and wet it. Then I bring it over to Johnny, who is now leaning against the kitchen doorway, still in his soaking wet clothes from the rain.

Where is Julie? I can't figure out why she isn't checking on Johnny to see if he's alright or not. I know she's changed a lot, but not to care at all, that seems wrong even for Julie to do.

As I hand the wet cloth to my brother he says, "I want you to stay away from that guy Rufus. He's bad news. Do your best to stay the hell away from him." Then he heads clumsily back up the stairs while holding the rag to his head, hopefully to change out of his wet clothes.

It's still raining hard outside. The sky is so dark, I actually have to turn the kitchen light on to be able to see what I am doing.

While I'm working on tidying up the kitchen, I hear strange noises coming from my old bedroom. I don't want to hear them, but I can't help it. Since the dishes are all cleaned, dried and put away already, I decide now is a good time to get the clothes from the washer in the basement. At least I shouldn't be able to hear the screaming and bed squeaking from down there.

I hate the basement but at least down here I can't hear what's going on upstairs. I hope that man isn't being mean to Julie. She's really nasty to me, but still, I would hate to see her get hurt. I lean on my tip-toes to reach the clothes that are in the way bottom of the washer. Then I head back up the stairs, hoping that the noises have finally stopped.

That man is just coming down the stairs. My eyes accidentally meet his and he smirks at me. I set the basket of wet clothes down and head quickly back to the kitchen. I don't like the way he looks at me at all. He pokes his head around the doorway and says to me, "Don't worry, Sweetie, I will be back."

I don't even look at him this time. I busy myself with bringing the bowl of vegetables from the counter over to the table. A sick feeling creeps into my stomach and I almost feel like I'm going to puke. Thankfully he leaves the room and then I hear the front door shut. A couple of minutes later I hear the truck start and then pull out of the driveway. There is still a sick taste in my mouth. I am really scared of that man. And why is he taking Daddy's truck all by himself? Did Julie give him permission to take it?

I grab the thawed chicken from the shelf inside the refrigerator and then a baking pan from under the stove. I turn the oven on and then place the raw chicken on the pan. I rub some garlic and onion around on the chicken before I place it in the oven to cook and then I wash my hands good like my mommy taught me to do.

The onion always makes my eyes sting and water until a

few minutes after I wash my hands. I like the strong smell from both the onion and garlic that sticks to my hands even after I wash them. That smell will be there for a day or two unless I use garlic and onion again before then in my cooking.

Once my eyes stop stinging, I sit at the kitchen table with the cutting board and a paring knife. The salad will look so pretty when I'm done. It always does. First I have to get back up to wash this dirt off from the vegetables. I always seem to forget about that part for some reason. I don't like washing the vegetables, but washing them is better than eating dirt or dealing with Julie if she ends up eating some. I laugh at the thought of Julie eating dirt. What she would do to me really wouldn't be funny, but the look on her face would probably be something worth seeing.

It takes me a few minutes to wash all the dirt from each of the vegetables. When I'm finally done, I sit back down at the table with them. I hear Johnny's heavy footsteps come down the stairs. He peeks his head around so he can see me and says, "I'm going to take a hot bath. Are you okay out there?"

"Everything's fine. That guy left with Daddy's, I mean the, truck." I look for Johnny's reaction to this. I can tell by his face that he's not happy. "Are you okay," I ask, referring to his bleeding head and black eye.

"I'll be fine and I know about him leaving with the truck. Don't worry about it. Just stay clear of him and Julie as best as you can." He walks away and then I hear the door to the bathroom shut.

Sure, that's easy for him to say, "Stay clear." He can take off wherever and whenever to do this and that or whatever he wants to do . I'm stuck here doing whatever Julie might possibly want me to. Even if I'm not right in the house, I have to come when she hollers for me or she'll kick my butt. So I can't really stay completely clear of her, not without ending up having to pay a big price.

Julie says that we have to keep up appearances so that I don't get taken away. Who cares if I get taken away? I don't really care what happens to me anymore. Life is miserable and everyone would be better off if I weren't around. Julie and Johnny would each be free to do whatever they wanted with the rest of their lives, without having to worry about me and where I would end up.

Julie and Johnny both tell me that I could get taken away and that I could end up with really horrible people who only want me so that I can do work for them all of the time for free, or worse. That's basically what is going on now. I'm with my older brother and the girl that looks like my older sister, but doesn't act like her at all, and all I ever do is work. And I feel so alone.

I have thought about running away from home. That is the dumbest idea that I have had so far though. There is nowhere for me to go, nowhere to run to. Then what? I have nothing to look forward to and nobody that loves or wants me.

I accidentally cut my finger with the paring knife as I'm slicing a radish. I flinch at the pain and then I watch closely as the blood rises up and then oozes out of the small cut. I lick the blood and then I suck on my finger to help the bleeding stop. I learned that trick from my daddy. The blood tastes like metal to me and I find that I actually think it is strangely delicious.

Then, before I even have time to think about what I am doing, I bring the knife to my chubby wrist and cut. It stings more than I expect it to, so I stop in order to look more closely at what I have done. It's only a small cut.

The blood rises up through the broken skin in small droplets. It's so beautiful, the blood. I watch the bleeding for a moment longer, enjoying the way that it looks and thinking about how much power there actually is in blood. What if I just cut myself and let all the blood drain right out? I daydream about how I would probably just drift off into death slowly and peacefully.

Then I snap myself out of the daze that I seem to be in, realizing that I need to finish making the tossed salad before Julie comes down or Johnny gets out of the tub. I lick my bleeding wrist and tightly hold a dark cloth over it for a couple of minutes to get the bleeding to stop. Of course I rinse the knife too, just in case there is still any of my blood on it.

The salad is colorful and looks really delicious by the time I have the carrots shredded, the lettuce ripped apart, the radishes sliced as thin as I can get them, the tomato cut up, and the cucumber sliced. My fingers are sore though from holding the knife and doing all that cutting and peeling. The one that I accidentally cut still stings too.

Nobody will tell me tonight that the salad looks yummy

or that I did a nice job. They never do, they just eat and then we'll go through the same thing all over again tomorrow. I'll do the chores, the cleaning, and whatever else Julie can think of for me to do. I'll probably end up cooking dinner again too. Nobody will thank me for any of it or even notice how hard I worked or what a good job I did. But if I didn't do even one of the stupid chores that I was told to do, they, especially Julie, would most definitely notice and I would get punished.

CHAPTER EIGHT
Julie

I wake up naked and a little confused. Then I remember and the dream-like memory makes me smile. I lean up on my elbow to look around my room.

I can see the evening sky through my window. Even though the sky is already dark with rain, it's not pitch dark in my bedroom, so I know that it's not night yet. That means that I didn't sleep through the rest of the day, which is a good thing. I need to make sure that nasty slob finally washed the dishes and did the other chores that she was supposed to get done before Rufus comes back.

I push myself up with the elbow I'm already leaning on to a sitting position on my bed, holding my sheet to my chest to hide my bare boobs. I'm not sure why I'm hiding myself, I'm the only one in here. I take another look around my room, this time looking for the clothes that I had been wearing before Rufus and I made love for the very first time. I smile again at the thought of it.

Oh shit, that damn cradle is still in here! I didn't even realize it until now. I wonder what Rufus must have thought. The doll that I now call Emily is in there, all tucked in and covered up as if she were a real living baby. Hey, I can call the doll Emily if I want to. Emily always called her Julie, after all.

I didn't want to take the cradle out of the room after Emily's baby died. After experiencing the strong bond Emily felt with her baby, I realized how much I would love to have a real baby to take care of and love, one that isn't all screwed up like that baby was.

Now Rufus wants to marry me and start a family of our own with me. Maybe he'll want to settle down for a change and raise our family here in this house. Maybe not.

My mind is racing with all these new questions. How soon does he want to get married? Where will we get married? Will it be a big wedding or a small wedding? Will his family even want me... ugh, I need to stop thinking for a while. I won't know any of the answers to these questions until after I talk to Rufus. I definitely can't come at him like some crazy woman with all of my questions at once either. I don't want to sound desperate and needy, that's for sure.

Anyways, who cares whether or not his freak family wants me? Rufus wants me and that is all that matters. That is all that matters in the whole world at all. We belong to each other now. I gave myself to Rufus completely and now I am his. And Rufus is mine. All we really need is each other from now on.

I decide that Rufus won't care about the cradle being in my room. If he says anything or thinks that it's weird, I'll just tell him that it is a family heirloom. He will understand. Hopefully we will fill the cradle with a real baby of our own soon enough.

Well, I better get my ass out of this bed and dressed if I want to make sure Caroline did all of her chores for the day. I need to start making a list to leave for her. She definitely isn't good about figuring out on her own what extra stuff needs to be done around here. I don't think the fridge has been cleaned since Emily did it last. That thought is absolutely disgusting.

I should take a bath to freshen myself up before Rufus comes back too. Just thinking about him makes me smile all over again. I don't think I have ever smiled as much as I have today. I have Rufus to thank for that. I am so happy that I decided to check the fairgrounds today in the hopes that he might be there.

I know Johnny and Caroline think that I'm a bitch. I'm sure that neither one of them is very fond of my boyfriend Rufus either. That is perfectly fine with me. I don't stick around for lovey dovey family relationships. I couldn't care less about what either Johnny or Caroline think of me.

I stick around because I know that Caroline still needs me and because at least part of this house and land are mine. Emotionally, I don't give a shit about any of it, but I know the value of staying and doing my part.

For one, if I left and things fell apart, Caroline would end up in a home with strangers raising her. For two, if I left, then all of the Fleischer's deep dark secrets would probably become the talk of the news and all of the townspeople. Then I would probably go to jail along with Johnny for his, Emily's, and even my own role in everything that happened in 1976 and everything that has happened since. Plus, I know this house, barn, and the land that they sit on are worth a nice amount of money.

Mmm, as I slide my t-shirt back on over my head, I realize that I can still smell Rufus on the clothes that he took off from me earlier. Then I slip my panties and shorts back on, my boobs bouncing a little as I wiggle my butt into my shorts. My panties feel uncomfortably sticky and damp, but I'll wait to throw a clean pair on until after my bath.

As soon as I open my bedroom door I can smell whatever Caroline must be cooking for dinner in the oven. It smells like chicken and probably is. I had taken chicken out of the freezer yesterday to thaw but never ended up using it.

As I walk down the stairs I can see that Caroline is in the living room, hanging clothes on the rack because it's raining outside. What a hopeless idiot she is.

"Why would you do a load of wash when any moron could tell that it was going to rain out?"

She just stares at me blankly, probably too scared to even be able to think of what to say. Fuckin' baby. Before I have a chance to smack her or yell at her, Johnny walks around the corner and into the room. He smells freshly bathed.

"Just leave her alone Emily." He even has the nerve to look me in the eyes when he says this. Caroline backs away from where we're standing, probably knowing this isn't going to end very nicely at all.

"Don't call me that. My name is Julie," I scream at him, getting right in his face just to prove to him that I'm *not in the least bit afraid of him or of anyone else.*

"I know you don't act like her anymore, but I know that our loveable sister Emily is still inside the bitch that you force us to call Julie somewhere. We want her back. You've been nothing but a complete bitch and now you are a slut too."

I slap him as hard as I can across his face, making my own hand sting horribly. I can't believe he has the nerve to talk to me like this, especially after Rufus already put him in his place earlier today. What a dumbass. He'll pay for this. Either I'll think of something or Rufus will and Johnny will be sorry he ever even thought of crossing me this way in the first place, let alone actually doing it.

Johnny brings his hand up to rub at the cheek I just slapped. Caroline is backed as far away from us as she can possibly be without actually leaving the room. What a wuss. Both of them actually fit that description.

I decide to drop the matter for the time being even though I'm still fuming inside. I just can't think of anything good enough to say or do right at the moment. They'll both get what's coming to them in time.

"This bitch is going to take a bath. There had better be enough hot water left," I say as I walk purposefully back up the stairs to my room to get my towel and clean

underwear.

This living situation is not going to work out for much longer, I can tell. Maybe Rufus realized this too and that's why he is so set on going away to work with his family like he has always done. Of course, I'm not even sure that is what he plans to do anymore. We haven't talked about any of that since he asked me to marry him. So much is up in the air for me right now.

I go through the few measly items of pajamas and panties that are in my underwear drawer. I really need to go shopping for some new stuff soon. None of these panties are all that sexy. I don't really have the money, but I'll figure something out. I always do somehow.

When I get back downstairs, Johnny is nowhere to be seen and Caroline is still hanging clothes up to dry. Caroline doesn't look at me but says, "Dinner should be ready by the time you get out of the tub." I don't even respond to her statement before I walk into the bathroom and shut the door closed behind me.

Hopefully Rufus comes back soon. I don't like that the truck's not here if I want to take off for a while. I feel trapped and I do not care for that at all. The hot bath feels wonderful on my bare skin as I slide slowly into the bubbles. Time to drown out all of my troubles for just a little while.

DERANGED

CHAPTER NINE
Caroline

The argument between Johnny and Julie was very uncomfortable for me. I think I would have rather had Julie yelling at me, or even smacking me like I know that she was about to, than Johnny butting in and trying to stick up for me. Plus, he had called her Emily! We both knew much better than to do that anymore. Boy, that must have really made Julie angry. I was really surprised when she just turned and left the room after slapping Johnny. I thought for sure something much bigger was going to happen. I'm sure she'll take what he said out on me later when he's not around.

Once they are both finally cleared out of the living room, I decide to finish hanging the clothes on the rack. Julie has such pretty clothes. In the past, I would get all of Emily's old hand me downs as she grew out of them. But ever since Emily decided she was Julie, I've actually been wearing bigger clothes than her. I can already wear some of the things that Mommy wore when she was still alive. Mommy's old pants are still a little bit big on me, but as fast as every part of me seems to be growing outwards lately, I'm sure even those will fit me soon enough.

Julie gave me a really hard time because she had to go out and buy me some sweatpants. That would have been pretty exciting, if she hadn't made me feel like such a horrible, fat loser for needing them. They were the first brand new clothes that I have ever gotten in my whole life.

Maybe if I stop eating everything else except for salad and vegetables, I'll lose some of this disgusting chunk. Then maybe Julie will be a little nicer to me. She has always been skinny, so she has no clue what it feels like to be picked on for being fat the way that she picks on me. It makes me feel like garbage, rotten, filthy, garbage that no one could possibly ever want. Which is exactly what I am right now, a pile of garbage that no one wants around.

Just as I'm hanging the last piece of the clothing on the rack, it's one of the shirts that used to be Mommy's but is now mine, I hear the bathroom door open. My hands start to shake, worrying about what Julie will do to me since Johnny's not around, and I drop the shirt that I'm trying to hang.

"Pick that fucking shirt up off the nasty floor. No wonder you have nothing nice to speak of. You don't know how to take care of anything. I can't believe you're still hanging those clothes. What the hell, you are so damn slow," she says as she walks past me on her way to go upstairs to her room. She has a towel wrapped around her hair and is wearing the same cut off jean shorts and pink V-neck t-shirt that she walked into the bathroom wearing.

If I tried wearing my dirty clothes again like that after taking a bath, she would call me a nasty slob, or something just as mean. I'm sure she doesn't think of herself putting the same clothes back on after a bath as being a bad thing in the same way as she does when I do it. I can't imagine that Julie ever thinks any bad things about herself.

I wish I could just fall asleep and never wake up. I pray every night, wishing for an end to all of this. Then I feel bad, I know there are people worse off than me and I know that God must be very busy taking care of all of the other problems in the world.

It just hurts so bad to have everyone that I have ever loved taken away. It hurts to be left with an older sister that thinks that she's someone else, and the someone else that she thinks she is hates my guts.

I don't understand why any of this had to happen. I am confused about why Emily is Julie now and why Julie hates me so much. I do not know why or how Eric had to die and leave us, or why Daddy did so many crazy things that year after Eric died. I don't know why Emily or Julie killed Daddy and I don't understand why Mommy basically left us that same day. I don't get why Mommy had to die and I still do not know for sure if Julie killed her or if Mommy hung herself. I don't know why Emily's baby died either.

Why is all of this bad stuff happening to our family?

When will it all finally stop or will it ever even stop? I'm just so sad and so confused and tired of things being like this.

I can really smell the chicken now. I think it's probably ready, or close to it. I better stop thinking and go in to check if it's done so that it doesn't end up getting burned. So I walk into the kitchen and turn on the light so that I can see. It's so gray outside from the rain and that's making it really dark and gloomy inside the house too.

Then I open the oven door, the hot steam blowing past my face. I grab the pan of chicken with my dishcloth in one hand, not realizing how heavy the pan was going to be. Quickly I catch the other side of the pan with my empty hand, owww! The whole darn pan of chicken falls to the kitchen floor and some lands on my bare feet, burning them to match the new burn on my hand.

I look around to make sure that no one saw what happened and then I hurry to pick up the sizzling hot chicken with my bare fingers and put it back on the scorching pan. This time I have the pan sitting on top of the stove so that I can't possibly drop it.

I check the chicken over for any small clues that it was dropped on the floor, but can't find any. I guess it is a good thing that I recently mopped the kitchen floor. I grab a platter from the cupboard and place the chicken on it before setting it in the center of the table, along with the bowl of beautifully colorful salad I tossed up earlier. Then I set three places.

Julie insists on sitting in Daddy's old spot, right at the

head of the table. Johnny and I both sit where we have always sat, because we know that's where we belong. Well, that's why I still sit in my old spot and I'm guessing that Johnny's reason for keeping the same seat is probably pretty much the same as mine.

Dinner is ready now. I call out to let my brother and sister know that it's supper time and then I start tidying the kitchen a little while I wait for them to come join me to eat. This pan is going to be a pain to wash, I can tell just by looking at it as I place it on the counter next to the sink. I decide that I should let it soak while I eat. Maybe that will at least loosen up some of the chicken that is still sticking to it. I'm going to have to mop the kitchen floor again tomorrow. The spilled chicken made it greasy. I wiped up as much of the grease as I could with the dishrag, but I can still tell that there's grease left behind.

I just finish filling the sink with soapy water that has a lemony smell to it when Julie and Johnny come through different doorways into the kitchen. Neither of them looks happy to see the other. This is going to be another uncomfortably quiet meal, not that the three of us normally ever talk much during dinner anyways. I set the pan into the water as far as I can to let it soak. Then I dry my hands on the embroidered hand towel hanging from the cupboard door before I take my seat at the table.

I'm only eating the salad tonight. The chicken smells so delicious and it's not going to be easy but, I have made up my mind. If I can lose some of this extra fat, I'm going to. Then Julie will have one less thing to yell at me for or pick on me about.

While I'm eating my salad I think about what I might want to put in the time capsule that I want to bury sometime soon. I think I'll write down all the things that have happened that I can remember on either a piece of paper or in a notebook, depending on how much I end up writing. This way the things that have happened are told the way that I remember them too, instead of just the way that Emily thought that they happened.

I think I should add something of each of ours to the box. It will be very daring of me, but I think that I should add Emily's diaries to my time capsule too. I don't think that Julie takes them out of their hiding space ever anyways, so I should be okay and not get caught.

I saved Eric's rock collection from his room when Emily was cleaning his stuff out of there after he died. I wanted to keep something that was his. I'll add that.

I'll have to sneak into Johnny's room to find something of his to add to the time capsule too. I have no idea yet what I will add for him.

Adding something of Mommy's and Daddy's should be pretty easy, since I sleep in their old bedroom and most of their stuff is still in there. Maybe I'll add a couple of those pictures that Emily wrote about in her diaries for their piece of the time capsule.

I wonder if anyone will ever find the box that I bury. I continue to think about the time capsule and the treasures that I will put inside it through dinner. I also imagine to myself who might find it and when.

I'm actually feeling pretty excited for the first time in a long time. I have missed having this feeling, the feeling of actually looking forward to something. It's nice for a change.

CHAPTER TEN
Julie

Caroline is beginning to remind me more and more of Emily. She must remind me of something that I can't or couldn't stand about Emily for some reason. Maybe it's only part of Emily that she's beginning to remind me of, the weak, emotional Emily that I had to take over for.

I was hoping Rufus would be back by the time dinner was ready. He's not here yet though. And what is Caroline trying to do? All she put on her plate tonight for dinner was some salad. The stupid girl is probably trying to put herself on some sort of a diet. Doesn't she realize that it will never work? She hasn't been skinny a day in her life and I really doubt she ever will be.

Oh well, let her starve herself if that's what she really wants to do. I'm not going to try to stop her. Besides that, I have decided that I'm going to keep my mouth shut around Johnny until after Rufus comes back. Then Johnny won't have the balls to treat me the way that he did just before my bath.

What the hell, this is pathetic. Where the fuck is Rufus? He has been gone for hours. I have half a mind to hop on the horse to go looking for him. It's too bad horses aren't allowed on the main roads that lead to the fairgrounds. Anyhow, I would appear too needy if I went chasing after him so soon. If he's not back by tomorrow, that will be a different story. He has my damn truck, after all.

I need to stop this worrying. Rufus said that he would be back tonight and I am sure that he will keep his word to me. He has no reason not to. Besides, it's not even dark out yet. There is plenty of night left for him to still return when he told me that he would.

This chicken that Caroline baked is actually pretty delicious. She sprinkled some sort of spices all over the skin and she must have poured some kind of juice in the pan with the chicken while it baked too. It's so full of flavor that my mouth is actually watering between bites. The skin has just the right amount of crisp to it too, just the way I like it. The bites of chicken mixed with the fresh vegetables in the salad are almost heavenly. Caroline doesn't know what she is missing.

I wash my last bite of moist chicken and crunchy vegetables down with the last of the milk that's in my glass. As I'm pushing my chair back to get up from the table, I hear my truck in the driveway. I have to stop myself from running to Rufus, the man that I have fallen so deeply and completely in love with. I'm so happy that I hardly notice both Caroline and Johnny stiffen in their seats, and I certainly don't give two shits about how they feel about Rufus. It's none of their damn business who I decide to be with or what I do.

Rufus lets himself into our house through the front door just as I am walking through the living room to let him in. Well, even though it seems a little fast, I'm glad that at least he is making himself feel at home.

"Well hey there, Beautiful," Rufus says as he scoops me up into his strong arms for a big bear hug. "So, did you end up having a nice nap after I left earlier?"

"Mmhmm, I sure did, thanks to you. I haven't taken a nap in I don't even know how long! I guess you really wore me out this afternoon." He laughs at this. Before I have a chance to stop myself and think, I ask, "So, what took you away from me for so long?"

Rufus gives me a disapproving look just before he jokingly says to me, "Now if I told you that, I'd have to kill you." Then he laughs. I find the laugh a little bit disturbing and I decide not to push the matter. I don't want to seem insecure. He was probably helping his family with something anyhow, so there was most likely no reason at all for me to get upset and cause a scene.

Johnny walks into the living room from the kitchen. Without even realizing it, I hold my breath as he passes, wondering if he'll have the balls to start something with me or Rufus. I can tell that he is very purposefully not even looking in our direction as he walks by us and heads straight up the stairs to his room.

I can hear dishes clanking against each other. Caroline must be working on washing the dishes now, what a good girl. I'm sure she heard at least some of the fight earlier between Rufus and Johnny, if Johnny didn't already tell her all about it. I think she'll be on her best behavior and work her fat ass off from now on, at least when Rufus is around.

"So, what's for dinner," Rufus changes the subject, motioning towards the kitchen as he speaks.

"Oh, you haven't eaten yet? I'm so sorry Rufus, I should have known." Now I feel bad for not waiting for him to get back before eating supper myself. I take his hand and lead him into the kitchen.

"I'm sorry I didn't wait for you. I thought you must

have gotten something while you were out and I wasn't sure what time you would be back. Do you like chicken?" I motion for him to sit in Emily's mother's old spot and then I grab a plate for him from the cupboard.

"Yeah, chicken is good. Don't worry about not waiting for me. I didn't tell you that I would be back in time for dinner."

Caroline doesn't look away from the pan that she's scrubbing. She's either starting to finally wise up a little, or she's just too chicken that she might get herself into some sort of trouble. Either way, I'm happy that I don't have to deal with her nonsense.

I make a plate of chicken and tossed salad for Rufus. Then I pour him a tall glass of milk and set it next to his plate before I take my seat near him.

While he's still chewing a huge bite of the chicken that I gave him, Rufus says, "I want to take you to meet my family tomorrow."

He must see me squirm uncomfortably at the idea of this because he quickly adds, "They've been after me to bring you around so that they can finally meet the young woman that I have talked so much about. They won't bite, I promise. They're not like they used to be when my mother was my age. You don't have to worry about that. They will all love you, just like I do."

I let out a loud sigh and then I say cheerfully, "Of course, Rufus. I would love to meet your family. I can't wait."

Yeah, I can't wait to get it over with and out of the way. Of course I'm nervous. I have no idea what these people are like or what they will think of me. I shouldn't care, but I do for some stupid reason. I'm just worried that maybe if they hate me, Rufus will rethink having a relationship with me. Oh well, I guess there is not a damn thing that I can do about it tonight. I need to just concentrate on this time that I have with Rufus and make it special enough so that he'll never want to lose me.

Rufus finishes eating his supper in record time. I don't think that I have ever seen anyone eat that fast. We even had a whole conversation as he ate and he still finished faster than I have ever seen anyone do before. I wonder if he actually even tasted any of it.

"I need to talk to you, alone," Rufus says. He stresses the word alone and motions his head towards Caroline, who is still busy washing the dirty dishes from supper.

"No problem. I was just about to head back upstairs to my bedroom when you came through the door anyway." I push my seat back as I stand.

"Are you sure your brother won't hear our conversation?" Rufus stands too. I think about what he just asked. I've never heard anyone through my bedroom door or walls as long as they were just talking. Emily used to hear her mother and father talking, but only as muffled sounds, and that was from right below the floor, not all the way across the hallway.

"I'm sure, as long as you don't shout, whatever you say should stay between us." I lead Rufus back up to my bedroom, where we just made sweet love only a few short hours before.

CHAPTER ELEVEN
Caroline

I really do not like that man being in our house at all. Daddy would never have allowed someone like him to hang around here. Of course, if Daddy were still alive, I don't think Julie ever would have met Rufus to begin with. We wouldn't be calling Emily by the name of Julie either.

It looks like Rufus might be spending the night here. He went right up the stairs to Julie's room with her when she went. I wonder if they're planning on having him live here now. I really hope not. Life is hard enough without adding him to the picture. I hope there is no more fighting between Johnny and Rufus either. I don't like to see Johnny hurt.

I'm sure if he were going back to wherever he came from tonight, they would have left right after he was done eating his dinner. It's getting late and Julie doesn't normally go out much after dark. Instead of leaving though, they went up to Julie's room, mine and Emily's old room. Julie probably will have to give him a ride when he does go home since she brought him here in Daddy's truck to begin with.

My fingers and hands hurt so bad from scrubbing the darn pan that I baked the chicken on. The cut that I accidentally gave myself earlier split back open again. I have those weird old lady wrinkles on my fingers too, from them being wet too long. I hate the way my hands always feel after washing the dishes.

With nothing more exciting to concentrate on, after I've finally gotten all the dirty dishes from supper washed, rinsed, dried, and put away, I decide to search for something to use as my time capsule before I go to bed for the night. There are several boxes in Mommy and Daddy's closet in their old bedroom. I should go through and empty one of those out for myself to use. First, I have to get my finger to stop bleeding again.

Then I have a better thought. Maybe one of Mommy's tins would work better as my time capsule. I will have to see if I can find one that will fit all the things that I want to put in it.

With Johnny in his room and Julie in hers with that Rufus guy, I figure I should turn out the kitchen light, leaving most of the house dark now. I forgot to turn on any other lights for myself first though and, being afraid of the dark the way that I am, I quickly flip the kitchen light switch back to the on position. I know I'm a big baby, but when it's dark like that my mind likes to play tricks on me. Scary images of my dead loved ones always flash through my head to fill the emptiness that the darkness leaves.

Once I'm safely in my room, the bedroom that my parents used to share when they were still alive, I close the door and lock it behind me. Nobody normally bothers me when I'm in here at night. It has been at least half of a year since Johnny even stepped a foot in my bedroom, but I want to be extra careful tonight, especially with that strange guy being here with Julie.

There was never a lock on the door to the bedroom that I used to share with Emily, though Julie added one to her door right after Daddy was gone. I didn't really see the point in her doing that, it's not like anybody was going to bother her anymore, but I guess it makes her feel better.

I like that there is a lock on the door to the bedroom that I have now. It's nice to know that I can lock myself in whenever I feel like it. I know that if someone was really determined to get in that they would still be able to and the lock wouldn't stop them, but it helps me feel better. Plus, it will give me the warning that I need to stop what I'm doing or, in a really bad situation, enough time to climb out my bedroom window.

There are some strange things in Mommy and Daddy's old closet, along with a stale, moth ball smell. There are tins of buttons and cloth, thread, needles, and other stuff of the sort. One of these will work perfectly for my time capsule and is easy enough to empty out. Finally, here's the box with the pictures and articles that Emily wrote about. I'll put all of these into the time capsule for someone else to find and put the odd pieces of our family history together for themselves, what Emily didn't already spell out in her journals, that is.

I went through the closet as quickly and quietly as I possibly could. Then I put everything carefully back the way that it was, except for the tin that I emptied of the cloth and then added the photos and newspaper articles to. I placed Eric's rock collection in the tin as well.

Now I'm exhausted and ready to sleep. Tomorrow I'll grab Emily's journals and something of Johnny's to add to the box as soon as I get the chance. Maybe I'll even be able to bury the time capsule tomorrow too.

I drift off to sleep with the time capsule I'm going to bury on my mind, not knowing that things would start to happen very quickly around here.

CHAPTER TWELVE

Julie

Last night after we were up in my room, Rufus had told me how he had heard on the news about the diner burning. The police were calling it an arson and looking for anyone who may have any information about who set the fire that killed thirty-seven people. Thirty-seven people, that is just insane. Rufus and I did that. We murdered those thirty-seven people because of one stupid, fat bastard.

Anyhow, Rufus had said that we need to get rid of my father's old truck as soon as possible. Which means that we will all have to go stay and work at the fair even sooner than I had thought. I thought we would have time to get things situated and make some decisions about things, but there isn't any more time to think. If anyone saw anything, the truck would definitely stick out in their mind and the truck would lead them right to the Fleischer's. However, if the truck were stolen a couple of days ago, all blame would rest on whoever took the truck.

So that is the plan for today. Rufus and I will head out so that I can meet his family and on our way there, we are going to find an out of the way place to dump the truck. It's all happening so fast. I'm a little uneasy about not having any time to think or plan, but I have known for a year now that Rufus wanted me to work the fairs and circuses with his family after he came back to town this year.

Rufus also thinks that we should put the Fleischer property up for sale. That's going to be tough to get Johnny to agree to. I'm not going to ask him his opinion on the matter though, I'm just going to tell him that that's how it has to be.

Anyhow, it's time for Rufus and I to head out. We have to get rid of this truck and meet the rest of his family. This ought to be an interesting day, especially since I'm not sure yet how we're going to get back to my house afterwards. Plus, neither Rufus or I got much sleep last night either. My bed is way too small and we couldn't seem to keep our hands off each other. Oh well, it was a great night and well worth being a little tired and cranky today.

Rufus and I didn't talk much at all during our ride to find a place to dump the truck. He turned the radio on and I turned the volume high enough so that talking wasn't really an option. I just needed some quiet time to think to myself.

Rufus hasn't said any more about us getting married. It shouldn't matter to me, we've already said that we belong with each other and that nothing will ever tear us apart, but for some reason it does.

Well, we're here, I guess. This is where we're going to dump the truck, in this swamp. We leave the truck just as it is sinking quickly into the thick darkness of the swamp, hopefully not to be found for at least a few weeks. Then we walk the last couple of miles to the fairgrounds to meet Rufus' family.

"We'll make this quick and then I'll drive my camper back to your place where we'll stay for the night. Then we'll leave after you've had a chance to pack and straighten things out with Johnny and Caroline," Rufus explains to me as we're walking along the side of the road, holding hands with each other.

We get to the fairgrounds and Rufus introduces me to his entire family. I meet his two uncles and their wives, his three cousins, and his mother. Most of them look fairly normal, except the one with the strangely twisted face. I have a hard time looking at him and keeping a straight face. His family seems okay and they don't make a big deal about meeting me, which is great with me. His mother seems awfully quiet though, and not too friendly. I don't think she likes me very much for some reason.

Rufus gracefully explains our plans to his family and then excuses us for the night. Then we make our way to his camper and head back to my house. We still have Johnny and Caroline to talk to before we leave tomorrow.

CHAPTER THIRTEEN

Caroline

After Julie told us the news about leaving the following day to go with Rufus and his family, I was blown away. I had asked her if I could stay at the house with Johnny, but she said I couldn't. Actually she had said, "There's no way in Hell that I would ever let that happen."

It was sometime in the afternoon when her and Rufus told us and now it's almost supper time. Of course, I made sure I started dinner earlier and it's almost ready. We're having stew. I'm not positive what kind of meat I took out to go in it, but hopefully it will taste good enough.

I gave up on the only eating salad thing right after I started it. It only seemed to give Julie more of a reason to laugh at me and make rude comments. There's no point now in losing weight anyhow. If I don't want to be stuck with Julie, Rufus, and his family of freaks, I have to do something to change things. Change things is exactly what I plan on doing.

First, I want to talk to Johnny. I have a question that I need to ask him and I want to say a proper goodbye while I have the chance to do it when we can be alone together. The last I knew, he was outside tending the animals. I think I'll go find him and talk to him before I set the table for supper.

After visiting each of the animals in my search for Johnny and saying my goodbyes to them, I finally find him in the chicken coop, shoveling out the chicken poop.

He stops shoveling to look up at me and says, "Hey Caroline. Do you need something?"

"Johnny, do you believe there really is a Heaven," I ask, really wanting to hear what he thinks. Johnny goes back to shoveling, probably realizing that I just want to talk and not wanting to look at me while we do. That's okay with me, I don't really want him to look me in the eyes right now anyways. I don't want to end up chickening out of what I'm going to do before Julie tries to take me away with her and that monster she has for a boyfriend.

"Of course there is, Caroline. That's where Eric is, playing with all of the other kids that died way too early." I smile at the thought of Eric happy and playing with a bunch of other kids. A tear falls from my eye. I can't wait to be with him and happy like that.

"That's a nice thought. Are you going to be lonely when me and Julie leave with Rufus for so long, Johnny?" My hands are laced together behind my back and I'm watching my foot make little circles on the ground of the chicken coop.

"Don't worry about me, Caroline. I'll be fine. You just worry about taking care of you and coming back home safe in one piece to me." He's facing away from me now. I can see him from the corner of my eye. I can tell that he doesn't want to face me any more than I want to look at him.

"I wish I could stay here with you Johnny." I walk over so that I'm in front of him and throw my arms around his skinny waist to hug him. "I love you and I'm going to miss you."

Now I'm blubbering like a baby. Julie hates it when I cry but I can't help it sometimes. She says that I wear my feelings on the sleeve of my shirt for everyone to see. All I can think when she says that is that at least I'm not mean and heartless like she is.

"Oh stop it. You'll be back home before you know it and you'll probably have so much fun going around from fair to fair that you won't even have any time to think about me or this gloomy old house." He gently pushes me back away from him, holding my shoulders in his hands so that he can look down into my face. "Okay? I love you too, you little mushy girl." With that, he gives me a noogy on the top of my head and sends me on my way.

Next, I decide that it's time to bury my time capsule. I've decided to bury it in the garden, next to Eric's and Mommy's bodies. I never had a chance to write my version of things down on paper, but hopefully people will be able to put most of the story together for themselves.

I walk into the house and grab the tin. I have to grab something from Johnny's bedroom still to add, so I head up the stairs to his room. Julie's door is open and I catch sight of Emily's doll, Julie. Funny how she must have liked that name so much that she chose it for herself. At the last minute, I decide that the doll needs to be a part of the time capsule. Then I walk into Johnny's room, quickly looking around for anything that would be a good symbol for him and his life. I decide to grab a lure from his tackle box.

Quickly I take my treasures to my tin. Then I grab the tin and peek out the kitchen window… all clear. Now I can bury my time capsule before it's too late.

CHAPTER FOURTEEN

Julie

"You know what we have to do, Julie Baby. This house is yours just as much as it is his and you are all going to lose it if we don't try to sell it." He brushes the hair lovingly out of my face and then places a gentle kiss on my forehead.

I love him so much and I know that he's right. I also know that I don't want to lose him and there is no way that Johnny will ever agree to sell the house and go with us. He already told all of us that he would rather die than lose the Fleischer property and be stuck in a camper with Rufus indefinitely.

"Come on Honey, let's go talk to your brother again." He takes my hand and leads me from my bed and out of my room. We don't have much time to convince Johnny.

We're leaving the house tomorrow for the last time.

Dinner smells good. I'm so hungry. We're having stew tonight, one of my favorite meals. Rufus and I walk past Caroline as she's setting the table. Good, it should be ready soon then.

"Don't fucking look at me like that," Rufus screams at Caroline after we have already walked by her. I didn't notice her looking at him, or I would have said something myself. How dare she make eyes at my boyfriend! Oh well, that's a fight for a different time. Right now we have to deal with Johnny.

We find him just as he's leaving the chicken coop with the shovel in his hand. He wipes the sweat from his face with the bottom of his shirt. Gross.

"Hey, Johnny Boy, gotta talk to you," Rufus starts in, not giving me or Johnny a chance to say anything before he does.

"What do you want," Johnny doesn't even try to fake being polite. He sets the shovel against the hen house and walks over to where Rufus and I are standing with his arms crossed firmly against his chest.

"Well, I want you to listen to our plan. This is how things are going to be. If you don't like it, that's just too bad."

Johnny unfolds his arms and starts yelling, "I'm not going with you and we are not selling this property. That's final. I don't give a shit what you say. I know why the truck's not here anymore too, by the way. So if you try to do something stupid, I'll go to the cops."

Rufus begins to argue with Johnny. That's when Johnny starts heading for the house, saying he's going to call the cops on Rufus and I for burning down the diner.

I run over and grab the shovel, even before I really have a chance to think about what I am doing. Johnny looks over his shoulder at me just as I swing the sharpest part of the shovel down towards his head. Blood splatters. I can't pull the shovel from his head. It's lodged in about an inch deep.

Rufus rushes over to me and grabs the end of the shovel from my hands. He finishes what I started and makes sure there is no question about whether or not Johnny is okay. Emily's voice screams inside my mind. Her precious older brother is dead.

Rufus tells me to go find the axe. My mind is drawing a blank. "Go grab your father's axe! I know there has to be one. Julie!" Rufus slaps me across the face.

This snaps out of my daze and I run to the barn to

grab the axe for Rufus. We are in this together now and I need to stay focused to be able to help him.

Rufus is chopping Johnny's body into a bunch of smaller pieces. He begins to talk to me while he works, "Did you know that hogs will eat anything? They will even eat a person, bones and all."

"How do you know that," I ask, wondering if he has done something like this before.

"My family has worked fairs and circuses for generations. I have learned a lot of useful information over the years." He continues to chop at what used to be Johnny's body.

"So, we just feed Johnny to the pigs and that will be it? There won't be any evidence?" I get to my feet and stand over Rufus and Johnny's many pieces.

"You've got it, Babe." Rufus stands and grabs the shovel again. "You might want to go check on your little sister while I do this."

Rufus doesn't realize that the Fleischer's aren't really my family, that they were only Emily's family. That would be too much to explain and he might not understand.

I walk slowly back to the house, knowing that

Caroline is probably already freaking out. God, I don't want to have to deal with her blubbering ass right now.

CHAPTER FIFTEEN
Caroline

"Johnny! Noooo!!!" I scream from my spot at the kitchen window when I see Julie grab the shovel and run towards Johnny. I run to the screen door, but by the time I get there it's already too late.

I don't dare run out to where they are, who knows what Julie and Rufus would do to me. I watch quietly through the screen, tears pouring from my eyes and my body shaking violently with the sobs that are escaping from my mouth.

That's it. The last person on earth who cared anything about me is dead now. I watch Julie run off and then come back with something in her hands.

She has Daddy's axe. Oh my God, no! I know what Rufus is going to do to poor Johnny, nooo! I slump to the floor, unable to hold the weight of my own heavy body anymore.

Sometime later I wake up in Mommy and Daddy's bed, my bed. I'm not sure how I got here. Then I remember seeing my big brother Johnny get killed. I don't want to be awake. It's still dark out, so I cry myself back to sleep, where I can pretend that my family is all still here and everything is as it used to be.

CHAPTER SIXTEEN
Caroline

I wake up in the morning in the only house I have ever known for what is supposed to be the last time, at least the last time for a long while. Julie and I are supposed to travel with Rufus and his family to another fair after we work the New York State Fair for a couple of weeks. Julie's planning for us to stay in Rufus' camper, I guess.

I begin to cry again. I don't want to leave my home. I don't want to leave Johnny, Eric, Mommy, or Daddy behind. I don't want to go with Rufus and I don't want to meet the rest of his family. Daddy would never have let this happen if he were still around.

My mind is made up. I'm not leaving. Nobody can make me. This is my decision and no one can change it now. I have spent years thinking about this. Nothing better is waiting for me in the world outside my home. I climb out of my parents' old bed and begin to get ready for the miserable day ahead. I wipe away the tears from my face as best as I can before leaving my room.

Julie and Rufus are in the kitchen, eating breakfast. There is a plate already made up with French toast, bacon, and home fries at the spot in front of where I sit. Johnny's place at the table sits as empty as Eric's and Emily's now do. I have to wipe away another tear. That Rufus The Jerk is sitting in Mommy's spot and Julie, of course, is sitting in Daddy's old spot as usual. All of our spots at the table will be empty for breakfast tomorrow morning. There will be no one here.

"Morning," I say to be polite in an attempt to keep things as pleasant as they can be while I take my seat. I keep my eyes on my plate, trying hard not to look at either of them. I don't want to end up dying in some awful way, the way that my poor brother Johnny had to.

"Morning sleepy head. I should have known you would wake up after you smelled the food," Julie laughs at her own rude comment and Rufus laughs with her, of course. She's always picking on me for being chubby. I'm used to it now and I don't let it bother me, well, not any more than it already has.

I can't believe that she would still pick on me like this with what happened to Johnny only yesterday. Emily never picked on me like this. I really miss the old Emily that used to cuddle me and tell me stories to make me feel better.

My sister is gone, just as gone as both of my brothers and my Mommy and Daddy are. I wonder if my Emily is with all of them now or if she is trapped inside her old body with the new Julie. I hope for Emily's sake that she is with the rest of our family and not with horrible Julie.

Julie and Rufus get up from the table before I'm done eating. I hear them say that they should start packing their things for our stay at the Fair. I'm starting to get a tummy ache already. After I'm done eating, I get the dishes done and out of the way. I don't need Julie trying to track me down to get me to do them. I don't want anyone to bother me, so I have to wait to make sure that everyone is busy before I go about what I need to do.

I know where to find the rope. It's in the barn where Daddy always kept it. I have been practicing how to tie it too. I have the rope all ready to just hang in the tree now. I had to make sure to do it just right so the knot doesn't come loose when I jump from the chair. If I do everything the way that I am supposed to, I shouldn't really feel any pain. That's what Daddy always said about chopping the heads off of the chickens. Once the neck is broken or cut, there is no more pain. The rope will break my neck and then there will be nothing. Then hopefully I'll be with the rest of my family again.

Julie startles me when she comes rushing back into the kitchen. "Caroline, you need to start getting your things ready to leave. Rufus wants to be out of here by two p.m."

"I'm going to do it now. It shouldn't take me too long. I don't have that much that I need to bring. First I need to do something real quick though." This is the truth. Even if I were to bring everything that I needed, it would only fill one suitcase. I don't have many clothes and I wouldn't need anything else except for my hairbrush and toothbrush.

Julie doesn't know that I won't be packing at all. I won't need any of my stuff where I'll be going.

"Okay, but make it quick. I'll drag your ass out when we're ready if I have to. I don't want to keep Rufus waiting." She heads back up the stairs with her bare feet and nice legs shown off by a pair of short shorts to our old bedroom, the one she's been sharing with that freak for the last couple of days.

He really is a freak. That's what his family does at the Fair, they run the Freak Show. He doesn't look weird at all, but he says that the rest of his family does. He told us that his cousin has no ears and one of his brothers has seven toes.

I walk outside through the screen door, looking around at the land and all that is on it as I go. I have spent my entire life here on this land and in that house. It's warm and sunny out. The sun feels so good on the bare skin of my arms. It smells like it might rain sometime soon. I really like that smell.

I come to the spot where Eric and Mommy are buried, the only family members that are buried at all. There is probably still some of Daddy's cut up body in the freezer, but I don't think that counts. I don't think of Emily's baby as family either. I never even saw his body.

I have something I want to do. I don't want to do the thing I'm about to do without saying some sort of good bye to the only family members that I think would care, or at least what's left of them here on this earth. My mind is made up. I'm done. I can't do any of this anymore and there is nothing better waiting. I want to be with Johnny, Eric and Mommy and Daddy again. I don't want Rufus to be the boss of me or Julie to hurt me anymore. I don't want to look at Julie even one more time and remember my loving sister Emily that used to be in that same body. I don't want to leave my home, or Eric's and Mommy's graves, or all of the memories that are here.

Johnny was not planning to go with Julie and Rufus to work at the Fair even before they killed him. He told Julie that he had to keep up with things at the house, which he had been right about. With no one to take care of the crops and the animals, everything will go to waste. Julie wouldn't let me stay home with him either. I had actually asked her when she first started to tell us about it. She just told me how lazy I sounded and would not even agree to think about the idea. Staying behind here at the house is not even an option now and Julie took care of the problem of keeping up with the land, animals, and house by putting a For Sale sign out for everything that the Fleischer's have ever owned.

Johnny is the only one that I would have worried at all about leaving behind. But Rufus and Julie made sure that there would be no one left here to worry about. Now there is nobody that I am tied to here in this life. I've thought enough. It's time to hurry up and do what I need to do before I lose my chance. Time is running out.

As I leave the spot where the graves are, I look toward the house to make sure that no one has come out. I mope my way to the barn. I open the squeaky door while making sure to lift as I pull so it won't drag on the ground or get stuck. It smells like fresh hay in here. Quickly now I grab my rope and the stepladder, hiding the rope inside my t-shirt in case I run into anyone on my way to the tree. I'm starting to feel nervous, or excited, or maybe I'm both. I leave the barn for what I hope is the last time, set the stepladder on the ground just outside, and close the door back up.

Now my steps feel heavier as I head towards the tree. I look back toward the chicken coop, remembering the last time that I had seen Johnny alive. At least I had gotten the chance to say my goodbye to him before they killed him. I make sure that there are no signs of Julie or Rufus either. I'm alone, which is what the biggest problem in my life is. I always feel like I'm alone. No one really cares about me anymore, not me as a person.

I reach the tree and set down the stepladder. Then I climb the tree so that I can hang the rope from the branch. It's not easy, not for me. Eric used to climb the trees all the time. This job would be nothing for him to do. My arms and legs are getting all scraped up and my muscles are aching. I guess that doesn't really matter, or it won't in just a few minutes. I hang the rope and then start back down the tree. Getting back down is even harder than climbing up. This has turned out to be quite a lot of hard work. Well, as Mommy always said, "Anything worth doing is worth doing right and it's never easy." This will be worth it. It had better be.

I decide to take one last look around to make sure that I'm still alone and then I set the stepladder up just below the hanging rope. I'm really going to do this. I am going to finally be free and there will be no more sadness and no more pain. I have to believe this.

I climb to the top of the stepladder. Starting to get shaky from being nervous, I realize that this is it. It's now or never. I bring the noose down around my head like I would do with a necklace. I have never owned a necklace. Mommy had some that were still in my room and I would sometimes wear one of them so that I could feel closer to her. There's no time for thinking about these silly things now. I quietly say, "Good-bye," and then I kick the ladder out from under myself.

And now, for me at least, it's finally over.

DEMENTED
BOOK 3 OF THE
FLEISCHER SERIES

COMING OCTOBER 2014

About Deranged

I'm Caroline Anne Fleischer and this book written by me is not the only one of its kind. I know this because I found and read the book that my sister Emily wrote. I'm not really much of a reader or writer, but I will do the best that I can because I want my part of the story to be heard too, before these ideas that I fight with in my head win and there is no more story to be told. I'll try to pick up where my sister left off, after the terrible things that she did. Now I know the truth about all of it and I'll fill you in on the horrible stuff that has happened even since then.

And I'm Julie, just Julie. Emily needed me to help her do what needed to be done and she needs me even more now because she can't deal with the memories of what we did. Now I'm simply doing the things that need to be done to continue to survive and make some sort of a life for Emily- or myself. Survival of the fittest, as they say.

ABOUT THE AUTHOR

Wendi Starusnak lives in Phoenix, New York with her husband, six of their eight children (the rest have grown and are living their own stories while still remaining strong characters in their parents' story), her mother-in-law, and their little dog that thinks he's a person. Wendi enjoys writing the darker stuff and hopes to be a voice against abuse. She began writing as a small child and whenever the question of what she wanted to be when she grew up was asked, she responded with, "a published author".

HOW TO CONNECT

www.facebook.com/AuthorWendiStarusnak
www.willowtree.b-town.us
www.twitter.com/@WendiStarusnak

Made in the USA
Charleston, SC
19 September 2014